The Cheater's Club

by

Stella Grae

Cover Art by *Teddi Black*

The Wild Rose Press, Inc.
PO Box 708
Adams Basin, NY 14410-0708
Visit us at www.thewildrosepress.com

Publishing History
First Edition, 2025
Trade Paperback ISBN 978-1-5092-6168-0
Digital ISBN 978-1-5092-6169-7

Published in the United States of America

Dedication

To all the ladies who've been tempted, who've come close, but walked away—except in your morally gray minds. I believe you.

Chapter One: Wide Awake

I'm wide awake again.

Collin is nestled beside me, lost in a deep, peaceful sleep, and there are things that I need to tell him.

I need to tell him that I found a dress—no princess bride for me, but a sexy, sophisticated bombshell look that we'll both like—and hell no, it is not white.

I need to tell him that Fielding has snagged a band for the reception. It's a little college punk alternative for my taste, but she assures me they can slow it down and behave themselves; of course, I have my doubts...in the best kind of way.

I need him to arrange the catering—cake, food, booze—everything. If we wait until my morning *and* evening sickness subside, I'm afraid I will be forced to roll my very pregnant body down the aisle in a tailored tent.

I need to tell him that I'm scared, too, that I often wonder whether this feeling between us can actually last, whether I'm truly, madly, deeply in love enough with him to make this work for the long haul, or am I in love with *falling* in love?

He needs to know that a baby changes everything.

It changes your days and nights. It changes your priorities. It changes your perspective of your partner. It changes your relationship. And sometimes, those changes deepen bonds and goals.

1

And sometimes…they just rupture the relationship.

That's what I need him to know.

The distance that can creep between people is like a specter, lurking around the corner, waiting for an opportunity. And then it pounces on your happiness, as if it were helpless prey, swift and devious. He needs to be aware, to be cautious.

And I'm pretty sure I need to get a grip because we're way too smart to get to that point. *Aren't we?*

But first, I need to tell him why I have joined the Cheater's Club.

****

It's Saturday—the end of week seven.

In the starry lavender dusk right before dawn, the house is quiet—except for Collin's heavy breathing. He spoons me, deliciously close. One of his hands is wrapped around my slightly rounded belly and the other has snaked under my shoulders, resting on top of the beautiful, full mounds sprawling across my chest. He is absolutely hard, grinding up against my ass; I push back into him, spreading my legs wider with every teasing stroke. His hot lips softly confess his desperate, passionate words right into my ear.

"I love you, Jenna—the future Mrs. Collin English, mother of my unborn child, and kinky soul mate."

I giggle, covering his hands with mine, watching them knead and push my tits together. "I still turn you on?" I whisper to him, curious about his thoughts on my newly expanding body.

"Hell yes you do! This isn't a dildo in my pocket, lady. This is my very own, hard throbbing cock that wants you, exactly the way you are. Oh fuck! Your tiny pooch is so hot and those tits fucking rock my little corner of Kinweld, Tennessee. And I love you! I am just so damn happy right now, Jenna! Thank you for coming into my life, for being my wife." He lifts my ringed hand to his lips and kisses it.

"I love you, too, and trust me—it's *my* pleasure," I moan softly, reaching down to touch myself.

"Yeah, that's exactly my plan—*your* pleasure."

I raise my leg and drape it back over his, letting him help me hold it up. His cock pulses against the small of my back, in time with the shallow shuttering of his breath. Forcing myself to wait for pleasure, I slow my urge to press against him, hotly lingering in his frantic hunt—his pelvis awkwardly bucking and searching for the door to my sweet pulsing, wet hole.

"That's right, baby! You found it!" I groan. "Now, go slow at first. Show me how you love to fuck it so deep and slow," I slur, intoxicated by his rhythmic drilling, which he is barely able to contain. He unleashes his passion on me like a torpedo, effectively burning away any issues I may have with my ever-changing body. He matches my wind up—moan for moan; his flesh pressed equally hard against my flesh; deep, strangled breath for deep, strangled breath. As I burst with a scorching hot satisfied heavy exhale and yelp, he grunts and pulls me against him, his hands cupping my tits, securing me to his body, as close as a tattoo. As his heart thumps against my shoulder blade, I listen to him haul air in and out of his lungs, trying to quickly recover from releasing his hot juice inside of me.

Collin kisses my cheek and pops up. "I'm going to jump in the shower, but can I fix you a little breakfast in bed before I head to the clinic? Maybe some of that nice homemade wheat bread we baked yesterday and an egg?" He traces my jaw with his fingertips, letting his gaze linger on me longer than it should.

"What is that look?" I quiz. "Is my hair all funny looking? Did you screw me silly?"

"No, your hair is gorgeous. I'm just thinking…what a lucky, lucky man I am. You are smart and beautiful, considerate, passionate, and we can talk about anything and everything. I feel like I can trust you with anything. When I look at you, I can see more than a great partner. I can see my past, my present, and my future."

The proverbial lump swells in my throat and I force it back down with a hard swallow. "I love you, too, Collin! I can't imagine things being any better." A pang of guilt loops around my words and I wish I could yank them back as I imagine life, with Collin, not pregnant. Quickly, I rebound with a diversion. "Do you want to know the one thing that would make this day absolutely perfect?"

"Name it—anything you want: anything you need. I'll do it."

"Some bacon with my eggs and toast."

"Ah! Now I know we're soul mates for sure. The lady is a meat eater. I'll be right back."

From upstairs, I hear the clinging of pans and consider how good Collin is to me. *Do you even deserve this?* The thought hangs in my mind like a looming storm, hovering over me, threatening to ruin a great beginning to my day. *Why wouldn't I deserve him?* I've waited a long time to have someone adore me like I adore him. And I do adore him, but I'm nervous about the baby, and Fielding's growing pains because they don't really match mine anymore, telling the kids about a new baby, and everything else…because a baby changes everything. Anxiety clenches me in its path and a new wave of nausea topples me. I turn to my side and breathe deeply, trying to will it away, but I know, there's only so much I can do to quell the flame of disorder that threatens all the great things I know I deserve and want...*I do want them, right?*

A light doze takes over and when I hear the rattle of dishes on the breakfast tray, I jump. Collin delivers my eggs, bacon, and toast complete with the last of the yellow roses from my garden. Carefully situating the tray on my lap, he gives my bump a gentle noogie.

"This is what you need to get your beautiful spring morning off to a good start, especially for Junior there." He points to my stomach and I almost can't bear to look down.

"Ugh! No! We are not calling the baby *that*—ever again." I nibble on a piece of bacon.

A laugh gurgles somewhere deep in his throat. "Madam, you are my baby incubator—silence!" He throws a hand up to my face and then deviously rubs them together.

I lob a throw pillow at him and miss. "Lucky for you I'm progressively minded and can forgive your ignorance...and I'm an awful shot."

"You think it's a girl or a boy? Is it similar to any of your other pregnancies?"

My other pregnancies. It seems like a lifetime ago, almost like another person was pregnant—not me. I think I was too unaware of what I wanted, to know whether or not I was happy. "Uhm...you know it's kinda tough to remember. I had morning sickness with all of them to some degree...definitely less with the last pregnancy. It's been a while. I suppose my body has forgotten."

"So, no guesses?"

"I'll say a girl. No particular reason other than the fact that I'd just like to have another girl. What do you think? You probably want a son, right?"

He shrugs his shoulders. "I think all men want sons, but a little girl, who's your spitting image? I'd love it, but she'll give me gray hair way too soon."

"Kids will give you gray hair regardless of their gender." I grab his hand and put it on top of my stomach. "I'm glad you're sticking with me. I don't want to do this by myself."

He lowers himself to kiss my bump, then my heart, my forehead, and my lips. "Jenna, you'll never have to do anything by yourself. Never. There's nothing you could do that would make me leave you. I'm not a quitter. I'm not going to be like my dad."

And there's the real reason he's sticking around. The involuntary thought racks my brain with disappointment. I don't doubt he loves me, but I'm old enough, experienced enough to understand that sometimes love just isn't enough. You need someone with sticking power—no matter the source. *So why am I so discomforted by that? Maybe I fear that reason will eventually fade away and maybe I fear that…it won't.*

"You seem kinda preoccupied. You feeling better?" he asks.

I perk up—for him—because he could never understand what this is like—forty is the new twenty. "I hadn't really planned on being knocked up at forty. You know?" I let the words plop and bounce out of my lips, hoping they land in a soft spot in his brain.

He lowers his eyes and rolls my ring finger between

his own hands. "I hadn't planned on it either, Jenna. Medical residency, marriage, a new baby—hell...a whole family, really—all at the same time? I knew—no, I know—I want all those things, but maybe not at the same time. But here we are. It doesn't mean it's any less of a blessing, it just means we're gonna have to work a lot harder to appreciate those blessings, yeah? You're gonna stick with me to appreciate everything we'll build, right?"

And he just gave me every reason to fall in love with him again. "Abso-fucking-lutely!" I laugh, shoveling a mouthful of egg. "It's a relief to talk about all this. I wasn't sure you'd get it. Sometimes I'm not sure I can do it."

"We can't stop talking, being us, being real. Just always be real with me, okay? Once you hit the second trimester you'll feel a lot better about it. Lots of changes going on in your body, in your brain right now, has you feeling unbalanced. And, once I'm a practicing physician, you can just stay home. You won't have to go to work anymore."

My head almost spins off its stem. "What the hell are you talking about?"

"I'll make enough money so that you can stay home to take care of the kids. You won't have to do it all. We're a team, remember?"

"Well, maybe I don't want to give up work...lose myself to domestic goddessing. Or lose that financial independence. You're going to take care of us—*all* of us? *All* of us? I can't ask you to do that. You didn't make *all* of this." I sweep my hand around the room.

Collin English squares up in front of my face and locks in his determined eyes on mine. "I will take care of you—*all* of you. You don't have to ask because I'm a man—it's what I do. I will not leave. I will give you a prenup if you want. I will be *the* man, the *only* man for you. I will be the man you deserve, the man you want, the man you need. Always, Jenna. *Always.*"

Always…as in forever. My heart is punch-drunk swooning, buzzing in my ears and sitting motionless in my throat. I can't even look him in the eyes. So I stare at the bacon on my plate, trying to keep a giant teary-eyed smile from turning into the awkward happy cry of the hormonally challenged.

"Hmmm…so is that 'Yes! I get to spend my life with the man I love' look or is that a 'Shit! I'm stuck with this schmuck for eternity' look?" he asks.

"You ought to know what kind of look it is. I'm happy, Collin." Half mumbling through a shaky voice, I watch as my tears drip on my toast.

"You sure don't seem happy, Jenna. Where are those tears coming from?"

I draw in a ragged breath and confess. "It's scary. Letting someone else have control petrifies me! For years *I* was the one…the only one. I never had to worry about anyone letting me down because I just held my breath and plowed through whatever I needed to do. Until now…and for the first time…I can let out a breath and relax because you've got it. You've got *all* of it if I need you to. I've never had the luxury of complete surrender."

He leans over and whispers in my hair, "Well, you better fucking get used to it because I'll make you surrender—*everything.*" He rubs his whole body against me, one long, taut, hard muscle. "Now, I better go jump in the shower before I'm late and have to renege on that promise."

I nibble on a piece of bacon, working up the courage to remind him of my meeting tonight. "You remember that I told Fielding I would go with her to her meeting this afternoon, so don't wait on me for dinner. I may not be home until close to six. I'll put it in the oven. If you get hungry, eat whenever you want." My tongue is poised and ready to parcel out the facts—only the facts he needs to know that will not arouse his suspicion. I condense my plan and my actions into one thought: *Is it impossible to be completely loyal while being scrupulously dishonest?* I don't want to lie to Collin, and I understand there are consequences to every action, even consequences for inaction, but my best friend needs me, and needs me in a way I'm not sure I understand. *Does sacrificing for my friend mean I might have to sacrifice my happiness? Is love strong enough to trump the intricately twined pair of truth and fidelity?*

"So this is like a counseling meeting for divorced people or what?" he asks, peeling off his underwear and shorts, tossing them in *his* dirty laundry basket, although he's been tending to *all* of the laundry lately. The hair on his head and his chest is growing back and he's getting that patchy road of temptation—the goody trail—that I adore, that I missed during swim season. It's almost as if Christmas has come early! His stomach muscles ripple as he turns and offers me a muscle man pose—biceps and deltoids popped out; they beg me for affection, for a naughty lick or two. Then, my eyes drop lower. The muscles in his thighs contract, forcing me to follow lower again—his calves. The plump balls of strength remind me of how compelling his body—and his mind—are to me. And finally, I allow my eyes to greedily devour his luscious tool, swaying free, tempting me and melting my reserve. I focus on his tight ass as he steps into the shower. Although my breakfast tastes good, my appetite dwindles, and I'm suddenly in the mood to be satisfied in a very different way.

"Jenna? Jenna? Did you hear me? Is this meeting you're going to like for counseling or something?" His voice echoes loudly over the water spilling across the walls and onto the floor in the shower, but I'm unable to focus very well on his question.

I slide the tray off of my lap and pull my t-shirt over my head, quietly pulling the door to the shower open. "I thought you might be able to hear me better if I came in here."

"Oh, yeah, that's an excellent idea," he sputters, giving in to my lips smothering his. His cock immediately comes to life and swells under my touch. "Actually," he strains against the pressure of my wet, soft tits against his chest, "this is the best idea you've had all day."

"And, the day is still so early and full of promise. So, to answer your question, the meeting tonight is like a group therapy session. Think Tupperware meets AA. I don't especially want to go, but Fielding asked me, and I feel like I need to be there for her. It's tea and snacks and gab—all the things we girls love. Well, all the things except for this." I pat the soap, getting my fingers slippery, and wrap my hand around him, stroking him gently at first, watching his eyes close and his mouth open, anticipating my idea for the finish. "Did I answer your question? Or, do you need more convincing?" I slide my hand to his balls, cupping them.

"Yeah, whatever. Just be careful and call me if

you're going to be later than six. Oh, that feels so good, Jenna." He lays his head against my shoulder, moaning. "Please don't stop, baby. You know how to make my cock come alive, don't you, momma?"

I quicken my pace, grinding into him. His hands crawl up to meet my breasts, lifting them to his mouth and tongue, which glides across my hard nipples. As I throw my head back and close my eyes, Collin dives into my jugular, licking and sucking my neck, a soft sensation against the bite of the water shooting out of the shower head into our skin like bullets. With my back against the wall, I pull my leg up, so ready for him to come inside of me. With the tip of his cock, he traces the pink ruffles of my mound, tempting every inch of wetness, teasing me, luring me to that precipice of having any self-control left at all. He reduces me to urge and instinct. Grabbing my ass, he pulls me to him and we moan in time with each other as he tunnels his way into me. His lips lightly settle on mine as we funnel our animal appetites into one singular moment when we bow at the knee and come together, barely able to stand after the waves drown us in satisfaction.

Resting his head on my shoulder, he kisses me, unsuccessfully trying to hide the huge goofy grin on his face. "You are something else. Shit! I thought after a woman got knocked up sex was over for a while, but you can really get it on for a pregnant woman."

"I guess that's what you call a hypothesis with hard evidence, huh?"

He laughs. "Yeah, I guess so! Listen, I better get myself together. I've got to be at the clinic by nine. I hope it's not too busy today. You've drained me—but in a good way."

"I'll fix *you* breakfast to go with coffee. How does that sound?"

"It sounds like my day couldn't get any more perfect!"

As I step out of the shower, I look back over my shoulder and watch his smile, watch him replaying the whole morning in his mind, and I think how perfection, unfortunately, almost never lasts.

Chapter Two: The Reward in Risk

At nearly three in the afternoon, a persistent rap jolts me out of my nap. It's Fielding.

"Bitch! I've been knocking for like five minutes! I figured you were sleeping and just didn't have the heart to ring the doorbell. Poor old pregnant mommy!" She laughs and pats my belly.

I reach out to swat her and snarl through a groggy yawn, asking, "Is it already time to go?"

"No, it's not quite yet, but I'm having second thoughts and I really need to talk to you." She paces back and forth in front of me, nervously running her fingers through her wavy chestnut hair. Her legs appear impossibly and impeccably long and lean in her tight jeans and boots. She is as visibly pained as she is beautiful. Her hazel eyes are drowning in conflict and her red lips beg, "Part of me wants this, needs this, even though I know it's wrong, it's risky, it could be the undoing of my life, but I need it. There's just something inside of me I need to explore, someone else I need to be right now. Jenna, please help me; help me figure this out."

Fielding plops down beside me on the couch, and drops her head in her hands.

"Fielding, why *do* you want to do this? There have to be basic reasons. What are they?"

She drapes herself across my lap, heavily exhaling

guilt. "This sucks. It's stupid. I'm being such a flake, a creep, immoral. I can't believe I'm even thinking about this."

"No, you're not. You're being very human. Just because most people *don't* talk about this shit doesn't mean it's wrong. Besides, there's a huge difference between talking about it and actually doing it. Everyone is tempted at some point, but that doesn't mean you're a bad person. You know I only want to help, not judge, never judge."

Tearfully, she gets up again, walking in front of me, then perching on the edge of the coffee table. Fielding digs out a list from her pocket and quietly begins. "I thought it might help if I wrote something down. I want to do this; I want to join the Cheater's Club because having sex with someone who doesn't really *see* me anymore is lackluster. It's become predictable and I can hardly muster up any anticipation for it anymore. And, I'm getting older, and it sucks because everyone who's *younger* notices it. I guess I want to know whether Cliff still wants me or is as sick of me as I am. Do I still have *it*? Isn't that what every woman wants to know?"

"Yeah, but at some point, you have to stop wondering and accept that either you do or you don't. That's not dependent on age, though; your sex appeal has nothing to do with your curb appeal. You practically bedded a freakin' rock legend for crying out loud! I think you've still got it! He could have had his pick of *anyone*, but he chose you. That's got to make you feel pretty damn good."

A sly smile creeps across Fielding's face and she twirls a piece of hair between her fingers. "Yeah, that's definitely in the plus column," she gloats. "But, the main reason," her voice breaks and she struggles to admit the words, "is that I don't feel special anymore. When Cliff looks at me, he looks *through* me; he doesn't see *me* anymore. I want him to get drunk off of the smell of my skin, I want him to tremble when I touch him, I want him to notice when I'm not around. I simply want him to make me feel special."

I watch Fielding's eyes trying to smile through the haze of tears. "You *are* special! You are so fucking special you don't even know it! The only person who might actually love you more than me is Cliff."

"Then why don't I feel like he does? Why doesn't he tell me? Why doesn't he show me anymore like he used to? We used to spend hours in a quiet part of campus, on a blanket, and we'd talk or he'd read poetry to me, or famous love letters. Why does all of that have to change when you try to make your life better? Is there only enough room in this life for love to be mediocre?"

I rub my forehead. "I thought after the reconciliation, you two were doing pretty well. What happened?"

"What happened is that old habits die hard. It took all of two months for him to stop going to counseling with me. And we haven't had a date night in weeks— *weeks*. The only things he's been dating are his solo bike rides and his existentialism journals. He kinda got me back and now it's business as usual—except in separate houses. What a farce! I guess mediocre is the best any of us can do in love, huh?"

"Have you talked to him again, told him you're frustrated? I mean, maybe he's a slow learner."

"Oh, fuck me, Jenna! Really?! I'm thinking if he's that slow of a slow learner, then maybe he needs a lesson he'll never forget. You know what I mean?"

"Ah, you're asking the wrong person. I've been the queen of denial for too long. I'm in the healthiest relationship of my life right now. Come back in a year and maybe I'll have a totally incomplete answer. Fielding, love has ups and downs, and sometimes it's stagnant. It can't always be exciting. You and Cliff have history. Isn't that worth saving? If that's mediocre, then…maybe I'm the momma of mediocrity."

"Well, if that's your best answer, then I think I need to go tonight, and you do, too. Did you tell Collin?"

"No! How could I tell him? I'm not planning on cheating; I don't even have a desire to cheat on him. I'm just going to be there for you, because you want me to go. That's it. I have my doubts, though. How can a group of people be trusted to keep a secret like that? I mean, it seems to me that the fewer people who know, the better. And, I'm no angel, but a club for cheating? That's kinda got a swinger eww factor, Fielding."

A silence lingers between us and I intuit where Fielding's mind is going because mine is already there. She turns to me and holds my hands. "I hate to put you in this position. I've already asked once, and that's more than I should have asked. So, I want you to know that if I do decide to do…something, I don't expect you to lie for me, especially if Cliff comes to you and asks. I'm a big girl; I can handle whatever comes my way."

"I know, but you understand no matter what comes your way, you'll not have to handle it alone. I'll go this time, but not anymore after tonight. I just…don't want to know, and I don't want to lie to Collin either, or Cliff. Please, you understand that, right?"

"Oh, of course! Of course I do! You know you don't

have to explain it to me, Jenna. I just feel like we're sort of veering in opposite directions, and I know I can't drag you with me down this road."

"But our paths will cross on the road again, especially if you cheat your ass off!" I laugh. "Just think, you could be forty and impregnated by your much-too-young boyfriend, too!"

"Ha! Ha!" Fielding throws a fake punch to my stomach. "Well, I haven't convinced myself that an extramarital encounter is the remedy—yet. We'll have to wait and see."

"How in the world did you find out about this cheating club, anyway?"

"A bunch of us at work were sitting around the lunch table, bitching about our husbands and boyfriends. You know how it is. The conversation moves from their dirty laundry on the floor to their moves in the bedroom, and the next thing I know, we're talking about what a fucking relief it would be to bang hot men in a meaningless sexual relationship—no laundry, no cooking, no pressure to be social, no kid issues hanging between the two of you. So, this one quiet lady, Laurie, makes the comment about how nice it would be to have a sort of cheating network. Of course, I'm all over *that* and blather on, and apparently too much and too enthusiastically because the next day in my work mailbox, I get a handwritten invitation. My full name is on it and inside, I pull out a linen notecard. On the outside of the card in large block print is WELCOME TO THE CHEATER'S CLUB." Fielding unzips her purse and the black block print, boldly drafts my mind to a dark, seductive place that makes my blood run icy cold. She studies my face and snatches it out of my hand, shaking her head. "When I open it these words are staring up at me, cementing everything that's been going through my mind, convicting me with the idea that this might *actually* be possible. The inside reads, "Everyone has secrets. And we're here to help you make sure those secrets never see the light of day. Join us for drinks and nibbles on Saturday afternoon, four o'clock, sharp. 754 Ringwood Drive. Ring the bell once; knock twice."

"That's really intriguing, but really odd, and honestly, kind of creepy."

"Yeah, I had goosebumps all afternoon, every time I read the note. I probably should have thrown it away, but…."

"But we're not the type to turn away from curiosity," I finish her sentence.

Fielding's eyes dart straight to me and she contorts her mouth with half a smile. "Even if it kills us."

"Well," I decide, accepting her help moving off of the couch, "let me get dressed and we'll see whether the Cheater's Club is worth it.

****

"Wow! I guess my theory about being tricked into driving to the bad part of the city has been shot all to shit. What do you think these houses are worth? A half a million?" I slowly spin the steering wheel around perfectly manicured streets buttressing brick and cobblestone drives. Spring has brought an early deluge of red and white dogwood flowers and crepe myrtle trees that hang heavy with blooms.

"Yeah, a half a million for the little five thousand square foot cracker boxes! These babies are easily a million or more. Did you even know this neighborhood was back here?" Fielding gawks out the window and rubbernecks on the view.

"No! How the hell would I know that? I'm an editor at an indie publisher. I'm lucky I'm still getting paid a decent salary in this economy. Shit! I hope we don't walk in and get raped for some snuff film or something!" I worry out loud, slowly navigating my car around the endless circle of fabulous homes, trying to find that one holding all the secrets.

Fielding throws her head back and snorts. "Oh! You're so dramatic when you're pregnant! If it comes to that, I'll go first, okay? Show you how it's done."

"Say, do you think that lady at your office, Laurie, had anything to do with your getting an invitation? Maybe she's in the club?"

"I've thought about it," Fielding muses, scratching her face, "but she seems so straight-laced, too normal for that kind of thing."

"Well, you remember what they say. You never know what goes on behind closed doors," I remind her.

"Yeah, I think that's the idea. Look! There it is, Ringwood. I believe you need to hang a left. It's 729— should be on the right."

I take my foot off of the gas and let the car roll to a stop. Fielding and I are confronted with a mansion, a gray stone Tudor hulk of a home, flanked by a snaking sidewalk of impeccably laid fieldstone. Lush evergreen trees and bushes surround the front and sides of the house, perfectly trimmed and shaped.

"I'll bet you twenty bucks that somebody does her bushes!" I seethe, simultaneously amazed and disgusted at the manicured state of the lawn.

"I'll bet another twenty that these aren't the only bushes that somebody tends to, if you know what I mean.

Ring the damn doorbell! Let's get this over with," Fielding snaps.

"It's not too late, Fielding. You can still back out if you want. Then, we can go home and watch trash TV and eat a whole pizza together."

Fielding slides me to the side and rings the bell, which echoes under the copper roof of the porch. She raps on the door twice.

A tall thin woman dressed in a short, black fitted sweater dress and tall leather boots answers the door. Her eyes are hollow and dark, and I can't discern whether their color is brown or something much worse. She is a brunette, except for the thick liquid silver strands of hair that fall over and around her face, with cartoonish-plump lips. Immediately, I do not like her, and I do not like being here.

"Welcome, ladies. You must be Fielding." She extends both of her hands to Fielding, warmly welcoming her with an indulgent smile. As her steely gaze turns to me, she spits out her question: "Who are you?"

"You can think of me as the cavalry," I respond, giving her cold eyes a run for their money with my own icy glare.

Turning back to Fielding, she lectures her. "Dear, this really isn't the type of party where you can bring a friend. It's strictly one in, one out. We have to keep our attendance numbers low, and reined in, for obvious reasons, of course." She lobs a look of intrusion at me.

"Well, I can't just leave her—I *won't* just leave her. If she's not invited, then I'm not going inside." Fielding stamps her foot and turns to me, hooking my elbow, leading me gently down the steps.

"Wait!" A voice from behind sternly commands us with less than five steps into our flight. "If it's that important to you, then she can stay. Of course, we expect the utmost discretion, and it's *only* because Laurie spoke so highly of you."

"So it *was* Laurie who sent the invitation?" Fielding gasps.

"One in, one out, and Laurie wants out very badly. Apparently," she continues, flamboyantly sucking in a breath of air through her nose, "she's patched things up with her husband and doesn't need our services any longer, so much so, in fact, that she's becoming a liability. I think it's time we have a new friend to play with, and I do so hope it's you—and *only* you." She punctuates her sentence with the same disdain that she used to julienne Laurie's decision to unrecognizable bits.

"We usually come as a package deal," I hiss, hanging on to Fielding, believing her life very well may depend on it.

She sidesteps to allow both of us to pass, stopping me in mid-step. With one finger in front of my lips she warns, "Remember, the utmost discretion—please do not forget. I'd hate for anyone to get into trouble, especially you."

I coolly sail past her and the biggest bouquet of white hydrangeas I've ever seen. I linger in their scent and take stock of my surroundings: crystal chandeliers, buttery soft leather furniture, Italian marble floors. I finger the delicate balloon-shaped heads of the flowers. "My mother had the prettiest blue hydrangea bushes. She would save up coffee grounds and at night I'd help her go out and dump them at the foot of each plant. It adjusted the acidity in the soil; otherwise, they would have looked like everyone else's hydrangeas—pink. My mother's beautiful blue hydrangeas drove our neighbor crazy with jealousy. You live very well," I observe.

"Yes, and I intend to keep it that way," she growls.

"Don't you find it ironic that something to be enjoyed, something so beautiful can be deadly?"

She glares at me, answering my question with nothing but silence.

"Oh," I point to the white flowers, "I meant the hydrangeas. The buds and the leaves are highly toxic. They contain traces of cyanide."

"Please, let's quickly find a spot. The meeting needs to begin soon." She ushers me into her great room, and I take a spot beside Fielding.

Facing her bisque couch, her beige carpet, and her eggshell walls is a white board with the following words: "If God doesn't exist then everything is permitted—Dostoevsky via Sartre."

"Hello, ladies, and welcome to the Cheater's Club. My name is Elizabeth—not Liz, Elizabeth. Like any good and proper club we have rules, and in this one, we live and die by the rules. Take a look around. These are your sisters-in-arms, your confessors, your saviors. Treat them well and honor the system, and you'll go far—as far as you can possibly let yourself fly. But, dishonor the system, and we will sacrifice you to your treason. No arguments, no discussion, no sympathy. I'll go over the rules and then we'll start with the introductions. I think it should be interesting. New blood always spurs on our participation." She nods toward Fielding and then turns toward a young woman, subservient and intimidated. "Amanda, are the refreshments ready for our guests?"

The dour-faced girl outfitted in black answers from

the kitchen. "Yes, ma'am."

Fielding and I follow Laurie to the kitchen. When Fielding gets close enough, she harshly tugs at Laurie's sleeve. "What the hell is this? What the hell did you get me into?"

Whipping around she checks for Elizabeth's patrolling eyes, then whispers, "I thought this is what you wanted! I'm helping you to be happy!"

"No, you're helping *yourself* be happy. You want out, right? That's what *Liz* said."

"Shhh! Don't ever call her that!" Laurie warns. "Listen, if you hate it, then you don't ever have to come back, but please, don't cross Elizabeth. You need to handle her very carefully."

"I'm not afraid of her!" Fielding puffs out her chest.

"Well, you should be. Let's stop talking before she suspects something."

As Laurie winds her way back to her seat, Fielding and I finish filling our plates and decide on a glass of tea. Its warmth and aroma comfort me; a cold chill trills up my spine as I turn to see Elizabeth staring at me.

"Are you enjoying the hydrangea tea? I made it myself." She puckers her lips together, trying to hide a smile.

"It's delicious," I purr. "The only other drink I've had that's this delightful is my own hemlock."

"You think you're very clever, don't you?"

Before I can formulate a response, she saunters back toward the crowd and I follow—but at a distance. Laurie is right: Women like Elizabeth do need to be handled carefully, and it's not because of Elizabeth's money or social status, but because she is wise to the point of being omniscient; she is armed with a brutal wit under which only the bravest test and survive. She is a gambler who knows what the lucky winner will never understand. There is no true reward without substantial, debilitating risk.

Elizabeth centers herself in the group and our eyes gravitate to her, giving her undivided attention. "I've told you who I am, and now, let me tell you a little about myself. I am your typical, jaded rich housewife who married as much for money as for love. From the outside we are glamorous and picture-perfect. The biggest lie is that I don't believe we even love each other anymore, but we're a little older, and comfortable, and maybe a little scared of being alone; we're very taken with our social status, and what everyone else is thinking, so we decided many years ago that it is perfectly acceptable to politely fuck other people. Unfortunately, a few of my friends were not so lucky, trapped in loveless, unsatisfactory, passion-starved marriages. So, ten years ago, I gathered together ladies for my first Cheater's Club. No matter how dirty the business may be, I fill a need. Why suffer through your life when you can happily fuck your problems away?"

"What about love? Fucking and love are not interchangeable, and simply fucking that one random person is never as good as fucking the person you love," I interrupt, challenging her philosophy. "I've done both and they do not leave you equally satisfied."

Elizabeth laughs. "Well, of course they don't, but you're not the only one here with a monopoly on that little revelation! What I'm talking about is operating on two completely different parallels. If you must remain married, and you choose to indulge, then you must keep the two separate. Jenna, no one here is naïve enough to believe that love and lust exist equally, or that they are equally sustainable. This club helps you deny your existence—a playground for grown-ups, if you will. I help you suspend reality, to make it more palpable, to make it possible to continue living. I can't create love! If I could, don't you think I would have chosen that for myself, and everyone else? That's a silly myth; don't trick yourself into thinking that love and marriage don't have expiration dates. Unfortunately, I believe they do. Now, I'd like to introduce my good friend, Landi. She's one of two original members."

Landi is very tall and very blonde; she is a perfect doll with brains because the first words she reveals about herself are, "I'm Dr. Landi Freeman. I teach biology at the university."

"Go on, tell the rest, tell the sordid truth that we all want to hear," Elizabeth encourages her, cradling Landi's halo of blonde hair.

"I am having an affair with one of my students. It's completely unethical, and it's not the first time I've done it. Though there is a physical component to all my relationships, my attractions are primarily cerebral. My husband doesn't really understand my work—the research, the writing, the desire I have to discover and dissect—he doesn't respect it. His repulsion of that side of my personality is only second to his jealousy-fueled disdain. If I try to leave him…I'm not exactly sure what he would do. He probably would try to discredit me; perhaps tell secrets that needn't be told. So, I choose this outlet—a frigging wellspring of fresh minds and thoughts, eager to learn and to please! In order not to feel too guilty about abusing my position and power, I mostly pick from the graduate students, occasionally a senior. I think some of my former students have a saying, 'Anybody can land Landi.'" She fake giggles and nervously chews at her finger; her eyes wander to Elizabeth for approval. "And, it makes me feel eternally young to be able to have this power—to attract the wandering eye of a man more than a decade my junior. I'm thankful I found the club. Otherwise, you'd find me curled up in a ball in the gutter somewhere—with bad hair. I never have to grow old or grow up or play the bimbo for the man who used to love me *before* I was a successful, brilliant researcher." Landi offers us a gracious, honest smile.

A lanky brunette sashays her way to the center of the circle and proclaims, "I love my boyfriend, I love fucking my boyfriend, and I love fucking everyone else's boyfriends, too, or husbands, or whatever. I'm just a horny little thing who likes to have fun! I'm an engineer—an attractive female in a male-oriented profession. So, like Landi, I've got a never-ending supply of male attention: I've fucked my male boss, I fucked men who worked for me and men I have worked with, business associates, guys at bars, married, unmarried, engaged. All it takes is that spark, that something to make me fall, to get me. I'm a helpless, lovefool—in love with falling in love—addicted to the excitement of something new, especially sex with a new man. I love making men a mess for me. It's the thrill of power."

"I thought you might start with your name, dear," Elizabeth restrains a cocky smile.

"Oh, yeah! That might have been more appropriate," the brunette's words bubble up from her gum-smacking lips, "My name is Michelle. Okay Shelby Lee, it's your turn."

A very pretty, very young woman with coppery brown curls plumps the crown of her hair and carefully steps to the center of the room. "I'm always so nervous at these meetings." She blows a thin wisp of air through her lips and touches her curls again. "Sorry, I'm a hairdresser; it's an occupational habit."

"And a damn good one," Elizabeth announces, her lips perched around the smooth edge of a highball glass full of something other than the tea most of us are having. "Go on, dear, you just go on and take all the time you need."

Shelby Lee's eyes fill with tears and with uncharacteristic warmth, Elizabeth walks to Shelby Lee's side and holds her hand, whispering something in her ear, which makes Shelby Lee smile.

In the momentary swell of quiet conversation, I turn and whisper to Fielding, "No doubt, Elizabeth probably recruited her in the salon where she gets her skunk 'do."

Fielding tucks her head to her chest and tries to hold back a laugh. "Shhhh!" she commands, swatting at me.

Elizabeth is quick to correct us. "Ladies, please! Shelby Lee has the floor."

"Uh, my name is Shelby Lee and I've been a member of the Cheater's Club for almost a year. I married my high school sweetheart and he's terminally ill. In a year, he could be dead, but that's what the doctors have been telling us for three years. Nearly eight months ago I began an affair with one of the hospice nurses who's been helping to take care of my husband, Johnny. I didn't mean for it to happen, but...he's been so nice and compassionate, making sure Johnny is always comfortable. And he knows a lot...about everything—

27

insurance, hospice, cancer, grieving. Johnny has melanoma. When he was first diagnosed, I thought the surgeons would just cut it out and go, but it's the terrible, aggressive kind that slowly eats away at him, so he's sedated most of the time. Surprisingly, it's not hard for me to be intimate with Chris; Johnny never sleeps in our bed anymore, so it's become a place for Chris and me now. Sometimes I think Johnny understands. I worry that he can hear us; his eyes are hollow and dull but he is peaceful when Chris is around, almost as if he knows I'll be taken care of. It seems I have been waiting for Johnny to die for so long. I can't go back, I can't quite move forward, and then there is Chris, waiting for me right here in the middle of it all."

With the exception of Elizabeth, all of us are teary, and full of understanding. If anyone doesn't belong here, it's obviously Shelby Lee. Laurie stands and gently guides Fielding to her feet, to the center of the circle.

"Hello, as you all know I'm Laurie, and I'm *leaving* the Cheater's Club. You won't see me again; I hope you'll *never* see me again. Things are good; no, things are *great* with my husband. I know some of you may not approve, or like it," she cuts her eyes to Elizabeth who is taking a long, thoughtful gulp out of her glass, "but love is worth preserving, and so is history with a person. So, per the rules of the club, one in, one out—this is Fielding."

Laurie gathers her purse and throws her jacket over her arm, quietly walking out the front door. There are no tearful goodbyes or explanations, or scandalous stories offered as penance, only the expectation that Fielding will fill the erotic, scandalous void. Fielding's eyes find mine and I have nothing to offer her, except an awkward, empty smile. She turns her back to me and begins.

"I'm Fielding, and…I guess I'm the newest member of the Cheater's Club. I…I work with Laurie, and she and I had a discussion, actually, a lot of discussions about marriage and fidelity. In a nutshell, I'm tired of having sex with the same person, and I'm especially tired of feeling like a useful appliance. Turn me on, turn me off—I have multiple uses, but none of them involve me being known as an individual—*really* known, really appreciated, and really valued, or validated."

I watch a few of the women shaking their heads in agreement and understanding. In the early days of love, no one expects to eventually be delegated to the position of bonus momma to her man because if the only type of sex you're having is perfunctory marriage sex, then this Cheater's Club is sadly alive and well.

Fielding continues, more animated and vigorously convincing than I believe is good for her. "I'm wondering whether this is all there is to life and to marriage? For better or for worse, I need to test my theory, and I can't think of a better way to do it." She quietly turns and takes her seat beside me, ignoring my eyes. Fielding and I simultaneously uncomfortably shift in our seats, acutely aware of the similarities we see in ourselves and in these women. And, the differences between us that have never been highlighted—until now.

Elizabeth carefully parcels out her steps to the center of the room, slightly slurring her words. "Now, I'm going to tell you the rules of the Cheater's Club. Don't forget them, and don't ask me to repeat them." She pulls out a small stack of simple white paper squares. We follow her words as she reads them from her copy:

"This club is based on mutually assured destruction.

Everyone who is a member is a cheater.

"There are no lies here. Here, you are free to be what you are without judgment. No matter how bad you believe you are or how badly you may have misbehaved, no matter your sin, we accept you and we forgive you. Bear your indiscretions to us without fear because we are just like you.

"Confession is good for the soul. Everyone has a story, and you will tell your story here. Whether it's to titillate, or to confess, or to justify, every week, every woman will share something. One in, one out. If you divulge our secrets, we will round the wagons and let you burn alone—no excuses, no second chances, no kidding. Fuck anyone you want, but don't *ever* fuck the club.

"Now…we're at the best part of the meeting, the part that I love the most—sharing. Some of you have heard this story before, but it is so very good, it bears repeating." Elizabeth's eyes glaze over and she licks her lips.

Michelle rubs the palms of her hands together. "Oh, you are going to *love* this. It is so hot! You'll have to run home and fuck the nearest vibrator."

"My husband is a pilot: very conducive to his cheating *and* mine. But, before I decided to partake in the fun, I was that pathetic, tortured wife, always wondering 'is he or isn't he?' So, I took matters into my own hands and booked a flight—*his* flight—to Rio de Janeiro. I needed to see with my own two eyes whether he was getting as handsy with one of the Latino flight attendants as I thought he was.

"Much to my relief, she was everything the other woman should be—gorgeous, young, sensuous, perfect ass, perfect tits, perfect hair and skin. I can see why he couldn't keep his hands off of her.

"While drowning my sorrows in mojitos, I notice a very well dressed Latin man staring at me. His eyes offer me solace, curiosity, buoyed up with an erotic undercurrent. With over five thousand miles to fly, we have plenty of time to eye fuck each other. At one point, he whispers something in the ear of his seatmate, who slinks his way to me and asks whether I would be interested in switching seats with him.

"At this point, I figure, who am I to say no? We drink, we talk, we laugh. I know, he knows, I can be had as soon as his fingers gently swipe my hair away from my face. A warm wave of familiarity washes over me and when I gaze into his eyes I cross a line over which I no longer have control. His fingers follow an imaginary trail, from my jawline, down between my breasts, below my navel, landing softly between my legs. He's very poised and natural, and we don't even have enough self-control to try and hide this white hot blizzard of desire that is building up between us. His fingers climb up my skirt and pull my underwear down to my ankles.

"As we stand, the flight attendant gives both of us a smile; he's done this before. Maybe I'm not his first, and I'm surely not the last, but at that moment, I don't care because I am having a completely selfish, totally perverse urge that is eating me alive, and winding me up inside like I've never been wound before. We shuffle our way to the flight crew lavatory. I smell my husband's cologne, which makes the experience all the sweeter. Before his lips even land on mine, I am breathless and weak, his fingers diving deep into my lovely spot, gratification roiling me to ignore any eleventh-hour sublimation. His fingers and hands are precise, delicately removing my clothing; I remember thinking I might faint—light headed and drunk off of the adrenaline. When he finally does kiss me, a spark erupts between us and my tongue winds across every inch of his lips and body. I clutch his shoulders and fall into him, trembling. He laughs and whispers in my ear, 'Are you scared?' I don't answer him because he knows what the answer is, and it is that, and yet so much more than an unfamiliar lascivious liaison. With both hands he spreads my legs, grinding into me, his eyes never leaving mine, and I surrender wholly to him. My juices are boiling, rolling in wave after wave; I let his cock impale me, sweet salty sweat running down between my breasts, which I wordlessly command him to lick. With red hot chemical desire overtaking him, I bend over the dressing table, spreading my cheeks apart for him. He tortures me with a prick tease, then, grabbing my wrists and pulling them behind my back, succumbs to his instinct and the only sound buzzing in my ears is the sound of his sweet hot fuck pounding in and out of me. With every muscle tensing and dancing inside of me, I succumb and his heavy breathing suffocates me in desire; we come together.

"My pussy is a wet mound of satisfaction and all the while dear hubby is working hard, delivering hundreds of people safely across the thousands of miles of deep, blue ocean. This is the revenge fuck of the century. His name was Eduardo—Edward—and he was the most beautiful man I've ever been with."

"It sounds like you loved him," I stammer, hanging on to her every word.

Elizabeth targets me with her eyes, but quickly dismisses her anger. "No, I didn't love him, but I believe

I could have. Although, I've discovered that the most successful romance is the one that remains quietly unrequited...because it lives in the perfect space of your mind, which is limited only by imagination." She paces back and forth in front of Landi and Michelle, her eyes rolling in mischief. "With permission, ladies, I'd respectfully like to request an exception to our rules; I want Jenna to come and be a part of our club." She slowly walks to within an inch of my toes and stands quietly in front of me. "I like you. You're a challenge to my balance."

"I don't belong here," I counter.

"Oh, but I think you do. You just don't know why yet."

Maybe I'm here to destroy you. The words never leave my mouth, but Elizabeth surely understands my heat of anger—and my cursed curiosity. I nod my head in agreement.

Even the cavalry has a weak spot.

Chapter Three: I'm Not the Only One

I helplessly sit cornered in my spot on the couch, desperately begging with my eyes for Fielding to rescue me. Instead, Elizabeth kneels in front of me, blocking my urgent communication.

"I want you to understand," she purrs, her hands firmly resting on my knees, "that I'm not angry about being challenged. You bring some valid points. I consider you a great foil to my demanding nature. Critical thinkers are an important part of the enterprise of infidelity. Of course, you'll have to abide by the rules."

Putting my hand to my forehead, I stutter, "I…I…No! I didn't ask to join. You invited me—I make my own rules…because I'm in a happy monogamous relationship. I won't do anything to risk it. I won't cheat." My breakfast swirls in my stomach and I wonder if I could summon its contents to paint Elizabeth the perfect shade of disgusted.

Elizabeth moves her hands from my knees to my stomach and I wonder whether she will do some sort of weird priestess of the altar shit and pull my baby out of me, bloodied, to sacrifice to the Cheater's Club gods. Her espresso colored eyes surround me with a giddy fear; she puts her face close—too close—to mine and whispers, "You've a child inside you?"

She smells like ginger, cloves, deceit, and pain—an

expensive potpourri of secrets and demons that are too valuable to let escape and too caustic to keep to herself. "I…uh…I don't know how you knew that? I'm not even that far along. Did Fielding tell you?" I press myself into the plush cushion, but she continues her invasion into my space.

She puts her nose next to my hair and hovers over me, taking deep draughts from my scent that treacherously floats around me. "I can smell it! I can smell the desire that made that baby. I'll give you six months—six months after that baby is born and you'll be begging to participate, love." She punctuates her prophecy to me with a wet pluck on my cheek. She rises to give Amanda undeserved shrewish direction in the kitchen.

With her release, my legs quickly deliver me to the powder room, dry heaving. My thoughts from this morning boomerang to me, mixed with Elizabeth's words, and I collapse to the floor, my head in the toilet, splattering the expensive porcelain with my vomit. I know I should clean it up; it won't be Elizabeth who deals with it. Pulling a much-too-big wad of toilet paper, I clean the toilet off and flush it, hoping it makes a clog that will hurt her bank account. *Heinous bitch.*

I scour the room for Fielding but the only thing I find are pairs of judging eyes. The massive round mirror in the hall reflects what I had feared: hair disheveled, face flushed, clothes wrinkled. *No wonder they're all looking at me. I don't belong here…for so many reasons.* I'm at least five or six years older than most of them, except Elizabeth, and I'm frumpy, swollen, and tired. I look at Michelle, Shelby Lee, and Landi—thin, long-legged with sexy high heels, generously endowed *without* the help of pregnancy, and dressed in clothing for appeal, not comfort. I can hardly stand to wear anything that cinches my waist these days. *You used to be hot like that*. I push that voice back into the place where all my thoughts, my concerns, my fears have been going lately. I don't have the luxury of reneging now.

Fielding's voice finds me before I see her. Her words are desperate and inflamed. "What do you mean you can't stop? It's not like you're in prison."

Shelby Lee's sweet voice is full of bleating tears. "I don't know what possessed me to think that this thing…this *group* was the right thing for me. Johnny isn't even really aware of anything anymore. He spends his days in an opiate daze, desperately trying to die."

"Hey…hey, hey. It's okay. You are not doing anything wrong. Not at all! Holy hell, Shelby Lee! Anyone would understand your position, and if they don't then they can fuck the hell off!"

I wobble over and strum Shelby Lee's back with my hand. "Johnny knows you love him. I think you're trying to wear a shame that doesn't fit you, Shelby Lee."

Fielding lays a vice grip on my shoulder and tears up. "This lady right here…she's right. She's abso-fucking-lutely correct, and the last person who'd ever judge anyone. Your secret is safe with us. We're your people, honey." Fielding smooths her last words with a touch of honeyed Southern drawl.

Shelby Lee only begins to cry harder at Fielding's words, and presses me with an oblivious glare. "It's not *you* I'm worried about! You two…you have no clue! You should just run out now before you do anything *really* stupid. Fielding, just run before you do something you can't undo, something that your husband can't or won't forgive."

"You'll go with us," I demand. The command comes from my gut, which is settled and full of ire for Elizabeth's heart traps.

"I can't! Elizabeth knows things. I don't know how she knows, but she keeps our secrets that she'll release like a hydra if you cross her. And that includes trying to leave without bringing in a new person. She knows things about all of us, things that can ruin us. I'm serious ladies...*run* before she can uncover your Achilles heel." A dribble of tears saturates and rolls down between her breasts nestled inside her silky blouse. "Please, just go and don't come back!"

Fielding puffs up and grabs Shelby Lee by the elbow. "Look, I know you don't really know me, but I have trouble taking no for an answer. And I can get kind of aggressive. Right, Jenna?" She shifts her weight toward me, searching for support before Elizabeth misses us, which I reluctantly give. "We're not leaving without you, and if Elizabeth has a problem with that, she can take it up with me."

"And that's exactly what she'll do."

A well-articulated response rattles me to swaying. I cling to Fielding and turn to a face full of Landi's blonde curls. "I won't tell Elizabeth what I heard, but if you're having second thoughts, Fielding, you'd better take your plaything and go home." Landi's eyes drop on me like she's covering some repulsive monster. "Shelby Lee, you know better. Stop fucking whining around and go find another player if you're unhappy. Of all the people here, it looks like you'd be the one who has the least to lose. What's your problem? You'll get your lover *and* the life insurance."

"You can go straight to hell, Landi!" Shelby Lee hisses.

Before my brain engages with my mouth, I utter the words, "I'll play. Shelby Lee can leave and I'll take her place."

Landi extinguishes her contempt on me. "Elizabeth already said she wanted you. You're in. Shelby Lee stays."

"If I'm in, then Shelby Lee is out. Elizabeth said it herself: one in, one out."

"I can't let you do that, Jenna! You're preg—" Fielding doesn't finish her sentence.

"She's what?" Landi demands, but releases our disagreement to find Elizabeth as we stonewall her.

Shelby Lee turns to me. "I don't understand you! What are you doing? You're going to have a *baby!*"

"How the hell does everyone know that?" My aggravation lands on Fielding.

"I'm sorry! It slipped out, but just to her." She points to Shelby Lee. "Who else knows?"

"Who do you think?"

"I swear to God, Jenna, I did not tell *her.* I would *never* tell Elizabeth. In fact, I don't want you to come back. You're done after today." Fielding crosses her arms in front of her chest and juts her knee out as if to block me.

"That's a huge sacrifice," Shelby Lee says, suppressing her excitement. "I can't let you do that for me. I'll find someone else." Shelby Lee drops her head and lets us circle around her in a hug.

"Huge sacrifices are our specialty," I mumble, nodding toward Fielding, squished into the safety of her biceps, wondering what the hell I'm going to tell Collin, and whether he'll admire my sacrifice or hate me for it.

****

"Jenna? That you, babe?"

Collin's voice is warm and familiar, comforting and gentle. *Don't be a piece of shit. Tell him.* Guilty waves pummel my resolve to cave and tell Collin about the Cheater's Club because of this one reason: I'm not going to cheat. I don't have to tell him *everything.* I'm sure he doesn't tell me everything. Maybe a nurse fresh out of college caught his eye at the hospital, maybe they had a little impromptu eye fucking adventure, maybe he even fantasized about her and whacked off at work. Would *my* life be better if I knew *all* of his secrets? In reality, a little ignorance is good for the soul. I don't think we're meant to know every intimate thought and detail from a person's mind. *That's keeping the mystery, keeping things in a healthy spot, right?*

I plop down on the couch beside him and rest my head on his shoulder. "Hey, Dr. Love," I whisper into the stubble on his neck, hoping he will avoid figuring out that the reason I can't make eye contact with him is because I can't quite look myself in the eyes right now either.

"How was the meeting?" he asks, shoveling a handful of almonds into his mouth, watching a home improvement show. Against the backdrop of the oohing and aahing over finding hardwood floors under layers of linoleum, I panic and clutch. *What exactly am I going to tell him?*

"Uhm…it's always interesting meeting new people. I don't know that I loved it, but Fielding could make a trip to the grocery store an adventure. I'll go again and decide."

Mumbling through his full mouth, he asks, "How was the counseling? What did you talk about?"

"Uh, what didn't we talk about?" There's a catch in my throat and I roughly cough, clearing it. "Like I said this morning, think Tupperware meets AA—people shared their stories, their struggles, there was food…games…" I trail off, proud of my telling of a half-truth.

Suddenly Collin grabs the remote and mutes the TV. "Is Fielding going to divorce Cliff? Because I thought they had worked their shit out. They're talking about living together again, right? Isn't that what you said?"

My heart races and suddenly I knead the palms of my hands together, trying to remember what I had told him. *Shit.* "Yeah, I think maybe they hit a snag. She's not entirely convinced she wants to do that. I don't know…she's having a moment. She'll be forty soon. Cliff doesn't pay enough attention to her. She feels lost. I told her she needs to give it time, give things a chance."

Collin canvasses me, an innocent curiosity blanketing his question. "Jenna, you're happy, right? I mean, if there's something—anything that dissatisfies you, you'd tell me? Because I've been thinking this whole time, why do you think you need to go to this with her?"

"I don't need to go except for moral support, babe! I told you it's a women's group. And I need…I want to support my friend. She needs me, Collin."

He pulls me toward him, reminding me, "Well, I need you, too. Don't forget that." He drapes my hand over his shoulder, turning my body toward his. "Let's go upstairs. I'm tired. I can rub your feet."

"And maybe I can rub something of yours," I tease,

yawning through my offer.

Collin scoops me up into his arms, and his hot breath wraps me in his promises of this morning. I scoop his jawline into my palms and kiss him softly, though not with passion—but gratitude. His arms and back are strong. He carries me effortlessly into our bedroom and gently deposits me onto our bed. *Our* bed. It's our haven, our safe space. He pulls my shirt over my head and scrunches my pants and panties down my legs, not with an appetite for anything other than the desire to make me see I'm the queen of his universe—forever.

"There you go, my love. You know you sleep better naked?" He grins, nuzzling deep into the fold of my ear.

"Said every horny man everywhere," I giggle.

"I'm gonna go brush my teeth, get ready for bed. I'll be right back." His kiss is quick and light on my forehead. And, I find it annoyingly paternal.

Sprawled out in the coolness of the sheets, I plan our words for the boys, Jacob and Bennett, about the baby. They like Collin, and appreciate his encouraging presence, but the engagement was enough of a shock. We decided that dispensing information a little at a time would be better for them. It makes me nervous, though…like I'm being dragged away from them, from the loves that I cultivated for so many years, forever loves that Collin hardly knows anything about. As much as I *want* to believe that this baby will bring Collin and me even closer, I fear it will make the kids feel like consolation prizes. *Can they ever understand and fully accept this new reality?*

Suddenly, I'm thirsty, and my head hurts. I slowly roll out of bed and navigate back downstairs, chugging two big glasses of water, and notice a bright pink sticky note hanging out of Collin's bag that's on the kitchen island. It's got blue ink hearts on it and swipes of feminine writing. Hearing the water still running, I eagerly spread the edges of the bag. Without disturbing its contents, I fish out his legal pad and flip to the page with the note. "I really enjoyed our walk today—thanks again for the coffee!" She drew a giant heart and signed her name—Lena.

Who the fuck is Lena? I let her name marinate in my mind. *Is she young and cute? Is she someone who's been on his mind? Do they have coffee on the regular? What kind of conversations are they having?* Suddenly, the Cheater's Club seems like a comfort. My pangs of guilt turn into justified, jealous stabs. It's one thing to just fuck someone else—dick in pussy, filling up a hole, fulfilling a physical need. But a *connection?* An emotional connection is much worse. In fact, it's a deal breaker. *Stop! You're being a hormonal jealous mess. Talk to him. You don't know anything about Lena.* But just for good measure, I rip the heartsy note off of the page and crumble it up, shoving it to the bottom of my purse along with all the wasted gum wrappers and old grocery lists. *I may not know anything about her now, but I'll sure as hell find out before I talk to him. Rule number one: Don't be a dumb bitch when you can be a smart one.*

A cruel truth hits me between the eyes:

I may not be the only one who's got a secret.

Chapter Four: Breaking Dishes and Burning Clothes

It's the end of week eight.

My phone pings me this morning at 6:30 with a frantic text from Fielding.

—Meet me for lunch @ 1230, can u do Thai?!?—

A quick self-check tells me my stomach can probably handle Thai today and I confirm 12:30 at The Curious Chopstick. I reach for Collin, but he's gone, already in the shower. It's odd he didn't hang around for our usual hot, sexy noodling and early morning pillow talk. *The note.* Its memory jumps the train track around my heart and pummels me with a familiar feeling: jealousy. While I'm not especially in the mood to get down and dirty, I am very much in the mood to get the dirty deets on Lena.

"Uh, calling Dr. Love? You ready for your scrub nurse?" I slide open the shower door and startle him. As he turns around, his hard cock sits in his very soapy hand. *Is he beating off? Is he beating off when he has a willing woman in bed right next to him?* I try to press these thoughts straight out of my mind, because he's clearly into me, hell…he loves me, I'm having his baby, and we've both been really tired lately. He's a doctor; he understands pregnancy on so many levels. And I'm a grown-ass woman. *Why do I not understand what's going on with him?*

"Mmm. I'm glad to see you. Can you tell?" The tip

of his cock nestles between us, throbbing and his face is pitted with drops of water. He looks genuinely shocked to see me in the shower with him. I think his response sounds too contrived to be genuine.

A heat builds in me and when I kiss him, I bite his lip, nearly drawing blood. This isn't passion. I'm pissed. "You have an early meeting? I missed you in bed this morning."

He rinses his face and tries to talk to me while he's doing it, so I can't see his face. "No, I just figured I'd get my day started. I still have a lot to learn, including when to leave here to get the best parking spot so that I don't have to sprint to be on time. That sucked yesterday!"

As he swivels his body back to me, I hold his cock in my hand and lower to my knees. "Well, *I* can suck today, then."

"Well, then, be quick about it, you dirty scrub nurse, you. Dr. Love hasn't got a lot of time."

"Are you telling me what to do?" I ask, the tip of my tongue flicking at the tip of his wet, hard cock.

He nods his head and pulls my hair back—hard— my head hinging backward until his throbbing dick threatens to impale me under my chin. "You like it a little rough? You want Dr. Love to cure what's ailing his little dirty cock sucker?"

I don't say anything. I just stare at him with water splattering against my face, unsure of this newly discovered rough side of him. *Maybe he likes it rough...he's never asked for it. Has he always secretly wanted it or did someone bring it out in him—someone like a secret lover?* I grab his cock full in my hand and tighten my grip, shoveling it in my mouth until I nearly gag. Willing it farther in, I keep the pressure around it and roughly pump it in and out of my mouth, not watching my teeth or putting my tongue in any particular position in my mouth for his pleasure. I'm fighting that cock and the whole damn time, drilling a hole in him, thinking about the note I found and the swirly feminine written name—Lena. He's wrapped my hair in another tighter twist around his hand, pushing and pulling me on and off his cock. His profanity-laced encouragement swells the lips between my legs until I slide my fingers on my left hand down for relief. Except the closer I get to finishing, the further away he appears to be from climax.

Tightly pinching his eyes together on his face, he yanks my hair again, threatening, "Yeah, I like fucking your mouth! I think your mouth and pussy were made for my cock. Keep it going, baby! Don't you fucking stop."

Collin pulls my hair even tighter. *Maybe I should be scared.* But…I like it, and I wonder whether he feels my same frustration at him taking an uncharacteristically long time to get there. I'm certainly not letting that stop *me*, though. My innocent groaning turns into feral grunting and moaning, and the delicate balance between my knees, toes, and ankles gives out. I fall on my ass and let the now-lukewarm water pound me with a realization that leaves me worried: *He can't come.*

Collin stands in front of me with his hard-on quickly deflating. He stretches out his strong arm to winch me up from the slippery shower floor. The space between us is awkward and the conversation forced. Quickly, a dozen reasons why a man might have trouble coming materialize in my mind. *He's crazy busy. This is a new job. He's concerned for me and the baby. There's been a lot of pressure to plan the wedding. He's still getting used to living together. Maybe he's feeling guilty...because he's attracted to someone else.* I let the last thought linger and ebb, then flow, racing from my mind to my heart, relaying one thousand times over again.

"At least one of us got off, huh?" He smiles after he lets the words sheepishly tumble out of his mouth, shuts off the water, and reaches for his towel.

I let my fingers linger on his shoulder and reassure him. "It happens. It's okay. Everything is okay, isn't it?"

He vigorously wipes the mirror with his towel and dismisses my concern. "Why wouldn't it be?"

"Life right now...it's a lot. I just...that's never happened to you before and..."

He finger-combs through his hair and I catch a glimpse of myself in the mirror. My belly has rounded to a pear shape and the slight dark bags under my eyes make me look every day of my forty years. My complexion is ruddy and I have a small constellation of zits on my forehead. "You know if you have concerns or fears, you can always talk to me. I just don't want you to feel like you need to keep things simple just for me. I can handle a lot."

"Yeah, I know." He shoves a minted glob of toothpaste in his mouth and brushes his teeth—intently staring at the back wall in the mirror to avoid my gaze.

I wrap my robe around me and turn back toward the mirror before I leave. "I liked the way you throat fucked me today. That was aggressive and hot and it made me completely come undone. Good thing I was over the drain in the shower."

Collin spits then hitches my arm in his and spins me around, landing a full-on heavy, wet kiss to my lips.

"You better like it because I think you've probably got a lifetime of practice ahead of you." He simultaneously swats my ass and grabs his clothes to get dressed.

I watch him pull on his pants and dress shirt, awkwardly fiddling with a tie. He furiously unfurls the crooked knot two times, cussing. He shoves his hair out of his face and we catch each other's eyes in the mirror.

"Need some help?" I ask, languidly tracing the bedspread as I make my way to him, slithering between his body and the mirror.

"I've never been good at tying fucking neckties!" he grumbles.

"It's okay. I can help you. I used to tie them for my dad. He had arthritis in his hands and it was hard for him. I got to be good at it."

"My piece-of-shit dad wasn't around to teach me how to do that—or much of anything else." He takes a ragged breath in and pushes it out.

I cross the edges over each other and needle the fabric through the knots I made. "Stick around kid, I'll teach you a few things." I grin at him, but he's not in the mood.

A dark frown overtakes his face. "I'm going to be late if I don't get going."

"Will you be home for dinner...regular time?"

"I'll text you and let you know. I think this may be my cohort's turn to pull the eighteen-hour shift. I'll let you know." He kisses me on the forehead and bounds down the steps.

Quick words of encouragement populate in my mind. "At least you won't be alone, I hope. Right? You have a colleague, right? Another student like you?"

He rips his ID badge from his bag and hangs it on

his neck, annoyed at my question. "It's a hospital. It's full of people."

I hang at his elbow. "I know…I mean, like…who are your colleagues? You never talk about any of them. I don't even know their names?"

"Jenna, I just learned their names! A lot of them are from other parts of the country." His eyes pop toward the ceiling, clearly in deep thought. "There's Sylvan, he's from New York. And Martine and Yvette—they're from the West Coast. Trenton from Texas, Quinn from Wisconsin, oh and Lena from Florida. That's pretty much my cohort." Collin quickly shoves a granola bar and an orange in his bag and squeezes my hand on the way out. He pulls away as I continue to hang on.

Instead of walking him to the car, I let the door slowly close on my words. "Bye, babe! See you later. I'll keep dinner for you."

Lena. Fucking bitch. I already hate her.

****

I finish my online meeting just in time to be late for lunch with Fielding. "Sorry, girl. Damn! Two authors and one manuscript—never a good plan. I'm just all over the place today." I slide into the booth side of our spot and Fielding is munching on a bowl of salted edamame.

"You should try these. I'll bet they're good for the baby." She points at my stomach, but doesn't look up at me.

I drape my hand over hers to stop her hand-to-mouth shovel. "Hey…I'm sorry. I didn't mean to be late. Okay?"

She shoos my apology away with my hand. "It's fine. I'm just feeling weird. You know, I thought today that we won't have too much more time together for

48

this—you'll be busy with the baby."

I slap my forehead harder than I mean to and exclaim, "Jesus! Fielding, are you pouting? *Really?* "

"Bitch, you know I don't pout. I was just being sentimental. Sometimes I just wish...I wish we could go back. Would you change things if you could go back?"

I nibble on some kimchi. "What do you think? Let's find a happier topic. Have you found your very own fuck boy? You can't disappoint the club." I bite my lip and grin, trying to keep from stoking my own jealousy at Fielding's new social calling.

"I did scope out a potential play area for us!" She suppresses a squeal, grabbing my wrists. "This is going to be hot!"

"Fielding!" I snap at her. "I've already told you...I'm not playing! I'm knocked up. There's nothing hot about going out with a middle-aged woman who's having her fuck boy's love child." I finish the sentence with air quotes because Collin is so much more than my fuck boy...*but that wasn't my intent from the beginning* I silently remind myself.

"Bullshit! You're glowing! Or, are you glowering?" Fielding takes a shot of soju as the server sidles over to check on us and bring more food. She whispers across the table, "Speaking of your young fuck boy...how are things? Have you told him anything about the club?"

As I pick from the obon tray between us, my eyes unexpectedly fill a little with tears that I try to will away with willful bites of the briny vegetables. And it's useless. I burst into an all-out snotting, ugly hormonal cry that progresses to my head dropping into my hands. I hear whispers and maybe even a few gasps. Then, a warm body and arms drape around me.

"It's okay, Jenna! I won't make you go to the sex club all knocked up." Fielding nuzzles my ear and puts her head against mine. "Seriously…what's going on, Jenna?" The only explanation I'm able to offer is more tears. "Ooooh, I see…you want to take me up on my offer for that ride to the abortion clinic after all, but you're too shy to ask?"

My tears turn to snorts of laughter, and when I look up, a few curious couples dot us with sympathetic eyes. "I think Collin might be cheating."

"What? Are we talking about the same Collin I know? No way, Jenna—no. You're delulu. Hormones gotcha good, girl. Uh-uh."

"Yes! Fielding, I found proof—sorta."

"Sorta is not proof. Now, his dick in someone else is definitely proof. That's what you have to have. Not sorta."

"He was super weird and distant this morning, and I caught him masturbating."

Her mouth rounds into a perfect O and both hands firmly smack the sides of her face. "Oh. My. God. A man is masturbating? Are you serious? This is definitely the kind of proof I'm talking about." She ends her sentence with a laugh.

"But he usually *doesn't* though. We've been going at it like rabbits lately. And I found something in his bag. Look." I pull out my phone and show her a picture of the note from Lena.

"Hmmm." She studies it and shakes her head. "This is definitely *something* but not proof of cheating. Maybe proof of thinking about it—*maybe*. Did you just ask him?"

"No! Then he'd know I was a snoop!"

"Well, women are…hello! A tale as old as time. You're having his baby, *and* you have a right to know what you're getting into. Just blame it on the pregnancy hormones, feeling unattractive, blah, blah, blah. It's a perfect cover."

"And he said it was his cohort's night to pull an eighteen hour shift that Lena is part of. Eighteen hours with *her*."

Fielding stabs a dumpling and holds it up to my mouth and I devour it. "And eighteen hours with *patients*, Jenna. He's trying to become a doctor, remember? He's at a hospital. Talk to him. Get the scoop on his schedule, his routine, his tasks. Geez…everyone likes talking about themselves. Just ask, for fuck's sake."

"I feel like a POS asking though, especially when I'm not being honest about our little club deal."

"Jenna, no one is 100 percent honest all the time about everything. You're not planning to do anything wrong anyway…are you? Because I'm pretty sure some guys, somewhere, are into that kink. And, you can't get knocked up if you're *already* knocked up!" She nudges me in my ribs and offers me a goofy little smile.

"No. No, no, no. Maybe he's just really stressed. I don't like mixed signals."

"Okay, so let's say he does have a little minor crush on a colleague. Let's say that's true, but he has zero interest in pursuing it. Would you really want to know that?"

I take a long time to answer because…part of me wants to know and part of me thinks I'm being hypocritical. *The Cheater's Club*. People find other people attractive. It's human nature. It's really no different than a celebrity crush, except she's much more accessible. And that's a big difference—accessibility. "I guess not, as long as he keeps boundaries—*strict* boundaries."

"Exactly. So, keep watching him, maybe do some more digging around in his bag as the opportunity presents itself. But I don't think you need to start burning his clothes and breaking dishes. Women and men can be friends and be supportive without wanting to bone the hell out of each other, ya know? Remember our friend Brian?"

"He was gay, Fielding," I remind her, rolling my eyes.

"Oh, yeah…bad example. Look, Jenna, Collin loves you—no, he *adores* you. He's got a lot on his plate. Give him some grace, but don't put your head in the sand and ignore shit, okay? You're definitely on the edge hormonally, too. Don't let all this go to your brain and freak out. That's a total turnoff."

"Well, so is being a liar, which I am precariously close to being. Talk about karmic energy. Damn! I hate lying about this. Maybe I *should* just tell him. You seem to be pretty keyed up. Where the hell is there a sex club close to Kinweld, Tennessee?"

She twirls some cold noodles around a chopstick and with a succinct slurp, giggles, trying to tell me through a mouthful of food. "It's in Nashville, so it'll have to be an overnighter, which is why I need the club—and you. You *have* to go with me. You can't tell Collin. He'd never let you go."

"Fielding, what the hell am I going to do at a sex club? And more importantly, what are *you* going to do…and do I have to watch?" I narrow my eyes at her and deep throat the last dumpling.

"I see you're practicing on that dumpling."

"Fuck you, you nasty thirst trap. Seriously, what are you gonna do at a sex club, Fielding?"

She throws her hair back and laughs at my patent naïveté. "So, *not* have sex—this time anyway. Obviously, you can have sex at a sex club, but just as many people go to watch. I want you to go watch with me. If I see something I like, I'll *think* about it, and catch some digits before I pull down my panties. Besides, I've kinda had my eye on that copier repair man at work. He's got the tightest ass I've ever seen. Dude's definitely been doing some squats."

I sigh. "When?"

"Huh? You mean I don't have to twist your arm, threaten you with a beating, or kidnap you? Seriously? You'll go with me?"

"And miss the scandalous good time to be had by all? We haven't had a decent road trip since the swim competition. Lord knows that turned out so well."

"Jenna, don't be dissatisfied. You've got a man who loves you to the end of the universe and back, a baby on the way who is so lucky to have you as its momma, three wonderful children who adore you, a wedding in the works, and you still look hot. I mean look at your titties! They're so full and voluptuous!" She reaches over to try to bounce one in her hand and I swat her away.

"Touch my titties and you'll go to the sex club looking like a character from some post-apocalyptic movie."

"So touchy! I kinda like the badass bitch vibe you got, momma, but save it for the club because I'll need protection from all the pervs who will be surfing around us. Seriously, your tits look great. Wear something revealing and you'll get a lot of attention, and soak it up because you may not be getting much of it for a while after the baby comes."

"Oh, you'll need protection alright—from me!"

"I *meant* since you'll be stuck inside with a baby latched to your boob, of course!"

"If I didn't love you, I'd beat your ass. This can only get better, right?"

"No, Jenna, it's only going to get worse—much worse. And I can't fucking wait." She grabs my wrists and squeezes. I involuntarily tighten my thighs, bracing for the tsunami of Fielding's imagination and desire. Watching her eyes glaze over in lust and excitement, I can't help but think she's absolutely, and unfortunately, a great match for the Cheater's Club.

****

At 5 p.m., I still haven't heard from Collin—not all day. I make dinner for the kids and me, direct bedtime, and by 10 p.m. I'm on the mental mess express. *Why hasn't he texted me? Didn't he tell me he would, or am I just imagining that? Is he with her?* As my mind scrambles to regain control, I hear footsteps. My newly minted teen daughter, Vi, is standing over me.

"Mom? Why are you still up? Shouldn't you be in bed...for the baby?" She combs my hair with her fingers, a move I've played a thousand times with her.

"Uh, yeah, I guess so. I was thinking I'd wait up on Collin, but...I'm not sure when he'll be home."

Vi studies me. "Mom, are you worried about Collin?"

"Well, no, but...." I stammer.

"This seems like Dad, remember? I remember you'd wait up for him, to make sure he made it home. This isn't like that, though, is it?"

I sweep her tiny frame beside mine and hug her. "I didn't know you knew that. I hadn't thought you'd remember. No, this is not like that," I lie.

"Yeah, I remember some of it. But mostly I remember how sad and worried you were. When I came in tonight, that's what it reminded me of. It can't be good for the baby to feel like that." She rests her hand on my belly.

"Vi, I'm happy, but relationships are hard. Love is complicated sometimes. We've got a lot of balls in the air right now, what with Collin's residency, the wedding. It's a lot. I'm sorry you noticed that, sweetheart."

Vi sits up and turns to me, offering, "I can help! I'm thirteen, Mom. I can do stuff—I'm great at planning parties, decorating, and I can make grilled cheese and scrambled eggs. That's one meal, right? It's not as good as a meal you'd cook, but that's a night off for you—and Collin." She stops and smacks her hands together. "I could help plan the wedding! Mom, I know I could do it! I've planned sooo many birthdays for my friends, and Hannah Schwartzklein's Bat Mitzvah, which was a *really* big deal. Do we all get to be in the wedding?"

I sift through the rapid-fire questions and comments, smiling a sad, satisfied expression. This young woman was once a babe on my lap and I thought we could conquer the world together. I just never imagined that it'd be this way...planning my second wedding with a baby on the way. I can only resist her pleas for so long, and I give in. "Yes, you can help plan, but school comes first. Fielding is doing most of it, but she's only secured the band so far. We still need a venue, flowers, a theme, colors...I guess. I don't want to go overboard, but it needs to be nice. This is Collin's first wedding, and I'm…." I stop myself from saying what makes me feel like a woman of ill repute.

Vi grins and reassures me. "It's okay. I know. Two girls from school just found out that their parents *had* to get married. All this time…they were lied to. I'm glad you and Collin aren't liars like that. I think that's kinda bad to do that to your kids." Her expression turns animated and she adds, "Guess what? I'm going to take a nursing exploratory class next quarter. Collin has kinda given me some medical inspo!"

"Really?! Vi, that's so awesome! I'm so proud of you! You've really got motivation and such intelligence." I gather her in my arms, hugging her until I think that my insides might combust from happiness. "I know Collin would be proud, too…to know that he had an influence." A sudden pang of worry hits me and I tear up again.

"Moooom! It's not that big a deal! You're so mushy like that." Vi rolls her eyes and says, "What's wrong with you tonight?"

"I…it's just hard with Collin being gone, and I know it's only going to be more and more. I love him, but—."

Vi cuts me off. "But you're afraid he might be like Dad—hard to trust. That's what's worrying you, right? That's the look, the one I remember."

I don't offer any reply to Vi other than resting my head on hers in another long bear hug, knowing that this young woman I'm raising will be so much more ahead of where I was—aloof, naïve, uncertain—at her age. *You're a lucky, lucky woman. Don't do something stupid to screw this up. Quit the club before karma gets you.*

"Mom," Vi clamps her soft hands around my face,

"if you love each other, then why worry? You can't stalk him. So, you're just gonna have to trust him."

I wake every hour, on the hour, always thinking about Vi's words, and finally at nearly 4 a.m. I hear the lock flip on the door and soon feel Collin's warm breath and body next to mine. In my brain, I count eighteen hours from 9 a.m. to 3 a.m. Then, I account for breaks and commute time. *He's home when he's supposed to be. Maybe I can trust him.* I snuggle up next to Collin and consider asking him how his day was, but that seems stupid. It was long and tiresome, judging by the way his snores sound like the Chicago L. The urge to pee hits me, followed closely by the urge to snoop. I tiptoe downstairs and find Collin's bag indiscriminately thrown on the couch. Slowly unzipping it, I find a small hand sanitizer, his stethoscope, a notepad with his printed name—*Dr. Collin English*—and a receipt from the Coffee Barn: two coffees, one black and one sugar and cream...*I've never seen Collin drink anything except black coffee;* two breakfast biscuits, one with no meat, extra egg. *My man is a meat eater,* I think...*and maybe he's a cheat, too. Maybe I* can't *trust him.* Grabbing the receipt, I tear them up into several small pieces and throw them in the garbage. I stomp up the stairs and throw my side of the covers back, giving zero shits if I wake him, which of course I don't because he's dead to the world. *If he's cheating, he'll wish he were dead.* And just as suddenly as the thought hits, I release it into the universe, only to reel it back in as a stroke of genius: *Maybe the Cheater's Club works both ways?*

Chapter Five: Cocktails and Confessions

Collin and I miss each other the next day—I have an early morning client meeting and he is sleeping in until his twelve-hour shift begins at noon. It's Friday and the Cheater's Club is in full swing, Elizabeth summons us for our regular cocktails and confessions themed party. A little before lunch, I grab my phone and type a quick text to Collin, including an "I love you" and hearts with heart-faced emojis, but don't hit send. *You don't want to wake him up.* I justify my hesitation, knowing good and well that's not why I'm not sending it. *Do I really love him...and like him...and respect him enough to change my life for him?* I don't hear from him all day. And, he doesn't hear from me. *Don't be so fucking immature.* More like, *don't be so fucking desperate to think you have to shoulder all the responsibility of sustaining a relationship.*

I beg off early, as it's slow, and my energy hasn't hit its stride yet. The kids are with their father for the weekend, and I'm enjoying an empty house. It won't be this way in a few months. I'll have sleepless nights, diaper changes, and a baby on my tit 24/7. Suddenly, I feel very stupid; I realize that Collin will probably still be working his crazy shifts and in full-swing of developing his career, his practice...*his* life. *The house could feel a lot emptier, and a lot lonelier. And what about my life? I had plans, dreams, hopes...what happens to those?* The growl of an engine jolts me out of a realization that I'd like to escape anyway. Fielding is driving this week and her horn blares over my thoughts. It's Michelle's week to share and I'm sure it's going to be juicy. Because she's the one most like Elizabeth— least likely to give two fucks about hurting anyone as long as she's getting what she needs, and especially what she wants. *And maybe I could learn a quick lesson or two about putting myself first.*

"Well, you look a little less like death this week. How are you?" Fielding asks, fidgeting with her heel and prying it off. "Shit! I can't drive in these damn things. I don't know how they all do it."

Through a sigh, I decide to fake it; no one wants to entertain a constant complainer. "I'm pretty good. Still a little tired, but feeling better."

Fielding plies me with disbelief. She slams the gear shift back into park and turns off the car. "I'm calling bullshit on that. You are *not* fine, and I know why. You're worried about Collin and you're worried about being a mommy—again. Jenna, dammit, you are not alone. Let me say it again: You are *not* alone! No matter what shit comes your way, I'll be right there beside you with my mop and my t-shirt: 'Let's Clean Up Some Shit.' I don't truly believe that Collin is cheating, but if he is, I will personally fuck up his shit for you. I mean, I will spare him no torture. I will—"

"Fielding! It's okay. I think I have a plan." She sits quietly and watches me while I study the dashboard display.

"Well...what is it? I've got a time limit in these toe-torturing shoes. Spit it out, sister, which is something I don't usually suggest." She winks at me and offers a fake

blow-job how-to with her hand and mouth.

"I'm going to ask Elizabeth to help me *catch* a possible cheater. She understands that I'm committed to seeing things through with Collin, and that I won't cheat. But, if she thinks there may be an opportunity for me to do some revenge cheating, she might be all for it. I need a middleman so I don't get caught snooping. I need to know that Collin is the real deal."

Fielding tests my forehead with the back of her hand. "Jesus, Jenna. Are you well? This pregnancy is eating your brain like a zombie. You're going to ask Elizabeth for help with your relationship? That's like gifting a serial killer with a brand-new set of knives and asking him not to use them for something bad. And since when did you ever think Collin *wasn't* the real deal? I wouldn't have encouraged him if I didn't think he wasn't good for you. Seems like there's something else with all this." She picks a piece of lint off my blouse and twirls my hair behind my ear.

"Maybe," I explain, ashamed to even let the words escape my brain, "I'm just not really sure anymore about all this. A brand-new baby, Fielding. I wonder if I'll live to even see him be successful and grown up and...all the things you want as a good parent. And what about Vi, Bennett, and Jacob? How are they going to adjust? A new baby needs so much attention." I let my words trail off and drop my chin to my chest. For a long time I thought I could handle anything life threw my way; I thought I could handle *this*. The only thing I'm sure of now is how life will never stop throwing curve balls, and how I foolishly once thought that fate isn't real. It's how you respond that matters. *Is that true?*

"Jenna, I know I joke about it a lot, but it's not too

late to have an abortion, you know. You have until about twelve weeks. I'll take you, if you want to go. I'll hold your hand. I'll help you tell Collin. I'll…do anything for you to be happy and healthy. If you don't think this baby is good for you and Collin, or for your family, you gotta do something. You can't just *hope* shit will work out. Where's my confident cougar momma, huh? Make some shit happen!"

"It'd be a lot easier to make that decision if I *knew* how all the puzzle pieces were going to fit together. But I guess I'm in control of that, huh?"

"Yeah, you are," she answers softly.

"It's nice to think of having a baby with someone who's actually excited about it, though. And he's great with the boys, especially." I shake my head and add, "I'm the queen of waffling. You got any syrup?" I laugh.

"No, but I got you on your plan. If Dr. English is cheating, we'll find out and take care of all the loose ends. Jenna, it's okay not to have everything figured out, and it's okay to make mistakes. Geez…you put so much fucking pressure on yourself to be perfect and to always have a plan. Relax, woman. Let life hit you between the eyeballs a time or two." She starts the car back up and takes my hand, holding it tightly.

"I already let life hit me and it missed…bullseye right into the 'ole twat."

Fielding parks in the driveway at Elizabeth's and scratches out a corner in her yard, leaving a fat wedge of bald, wet mud. "She needs to fucking relax all the perfectionist shit, too," she huffs, nodding my way.

As the door opens, the air is charged with the scent of lemons…*making lemonade when life gives you lemons. How appropriate.* I hear the star of the show,

Michelle, straining to keep her voice from lifting to the ceiling in a high, excited pitch, followed by a hushed tone that nibbles at my mind. *The sound of guiltless deceit.*

Elizabeth greets us with her skunk 'do pulled elegantly away from her face, which sparkles with the delusion of a woman truly tempered by others' downfall. She pulls Fielding to her and plants an air kiss on either side of her face. When she sees me trailing along behind Fielding, she circles my wrists with her bony hands and pulls my arms wide, examining my frame. "Well, you're absolutely glowing, Jenna! I do believe that an impending marriage and motherhood certainly agree with you. It appears we have many milestones to celebrate today."

A wild cackle of laughter explodes from the white-on-white living room. Amanda, the servant girl and likely keeper of the skeletons in the closet, passes close by, stopping long enough to offer me a canapé. Our eye contact leaves me with the sense that today's meeting will be...*perilous*. Fielding shoots me a look over her mouth full of fig and goat cheese. She makes a face and ducks into the bathroom to spit it out.

"Gym socks marinated in a basement. Ugh! What the hell is this vibe? Everyone is so freaking...*happy,*" she whispers my way.

"I don't know, but check out the white board sign for this week." *It's not manipulation if I engineer an agreeable outcome, even if you never agree to it. Elizabeth.*

"You're an editor, correct?" Elizabeth quizzes me, standing close to the small of my back, perched on my shoulder and whispering into the hair neatly tucked behind my ear.

"Yes, I am. And I think your wisdom is skewed. I have an editing suggestion."

I glare into the hall mirror at her, generously swollen lips smirking, deceiving, threatening me with her truth. Her face is tight and perfectly sculpted, belying her age. "What do you want from the Cheater's Club, Jenna? There's a reason you've returned, and it's not as friendly support."

A treacherous trill shuttles up my spine and I fiddle with the rough hem of my sweater. An effortless explanation flows smoothly from my brain. "I wonder whether my life might be falling apart…maybe…a bit. I want…some information, some help. The Cheater's Club might be the panacea I need to get things back on track, back under control.

"Ah! Yes, the burden of the traditional type A woman. You've liberated yourselves into submission with a different type of god—money. That puts you on the same plane with all the men swinging their dicks around, does it not?"

"And what about you? A woman's cheating club. Who's swinging her dick, now?"

"At least it's original. It's all mine." She pulls a lily stem from the tall arrangement on the hall table and traces my jawline.

"It's sad. That's *all* you have," I whisper.

"What's even sadder is that you're afraid of losing something that you probably don't even really want, do you?"

I swallow hard and break from her spell. "I need a spy and I might even need some bait. I want this to happen quickly." I let my hands fall over my stomach, resting them there, instinctively protecting what is mine. *What* do *I want?*

Elizabeth nods her head at me, tacitly agreeing to my requirements. "I'll take care of this myself." She slides the drawer on the table open and takes out a pen and paper. "Write down the obvious, important information, as much about his schedule as you know, and your number." Concentrating on herself in the mirror, she flicks her heel after a quick hair smooth, adding, "What was it…the correction you would have made?"

"It's redundant. Manipulation infers compliance without agreement. Here's what's missing in your quote—the word destruction. *It's not manipulation if I engineer an agreeable outcome. It's your slow destruction.*"

She pinches the tip of my chin between her fingers and shakes it. "I didn't come to destroy, love. I came to ignite and to defy." Her dark eyes flicker with a determined air of arrogance. "See, that's why I like you. You make me a better person."

Michelle's drawn out call to Elizabeth cuts our conversation to an abrupt end. "Eliiiizaaabeth! Where are you? Amanda's ready with the cocktails and I'm ready with the confessions!"

Standing alone in front of the mirror, my reflection appears pale and lifeless after my encounter with Elizabeth, and even more so now because the truth is in full-stop motion.

Fielding finds me and escorts me to a seat beside her, handing me a sparkling water. "Everything okay? You look a little pale."

I don't answer her. Michelle stands in the center of

our circle, glowing and relaying her exciting news. Elizabeth keeps her eyes on Fielding and me, and I am her captive. *Tied to the Cheater's Club, and ironically not for the wrong reasons.*

Michelle's left arm suddenly dives into the rows of eyes. A giant cushion-cut diamond ring on her left hand that looks like it must weigh a pound elicits an enthusiastic round of oohs and ahhs. "Dean *finally* proposed! I'm actually getting married!"

Landi snorts sarcastically. "I guess that means you'll be leaving the club?"

Michelle falls back on the couch, dramatically answering, "Oh, I'm just getting started."

Fielding and I exchange looks. I try to find Shelby Lee's eyes but they're plastered to the wall.

"Congratulations!" Fielding offers. "I'm sure it will be exciting to start a new life with Dean, do the wedding thing, honeymoon, the wedding gifts, living as husband and wife." Her eyes glaze over, trying to stifle memories.

Michelle blows her off. "Oh, we've lived together for three years. We need things like a new weed eater and a power washer. Not really terribly romantic. Good thing I have the Cheater's Club!" she exclaims, as if she's a model in a trite commercial.

"Why are you getting married if you plan to stay in the club? Why not just keep living together and…." Fielding doesn't finish.

A felon's smile plies Michelle's face and she seats herself next to Fielding. "Sweet, silly lady…you'll learn. Like I said, I love being that person who's etched on someone's mind—the power of it. I love lust, the pursuit. I'm not in the club to hurt Dean. I love him."

"That's an awfully odd way to start a marriage."

"Well, you're here. What an odd way to fix one."

Fielding sits up a little higher and leans her muscular frame into Michelle. "Bitch, you don't know shit about me or my marriage. And I've *earned* my place here, just like Elizabeth. I've spent tears and time on a man who can't seem to get his shit together enough to love me the way I *deserve* to be loved—after fifteen plus years of marriage *and* two kids. So, the only odd thing here is that you think you might even begin to understand my situation. Just get on with the entertainment, Michelle," Fielding hisses, grinding her teeth together, as angry as I've seen her in a long time.

As soon as Michelle stands back up in the middle of Elizabeth's cheating harem, my phone buzzes and I nearly jump into Fielding's lap. It's Collin. I excuse myself and find a quiet spot locked in the bathroom.

"Hey babe! How are you? I sent you a text earlier. You didn't get it?" he breathlessly asks.

A quick check of my phone and I clench my teeth together. *Shit!* The text is twenty minutes old…not enough to be totally rude, but enough that he was worried. I wish I'd seen it earlier; it would be easier to respond to a text rather than talk while I'm at the Cheater's Club. "I'm sorry, babe! I've been so busy and tired, just trying to get caught up. It feels like I've not seen you in…too long. How are things at the hospital?"

He exhales, frustrated. I can tell he's exhausted and his wits are frayed. "It's good. I love my work; that part's exhilarating, but…there's so much to learn, Jenna. I wish I could just collapse in your arms. It makes everything better. Are you feeling decent yet? It's week eight…almost nine, right? The sickness and tiredness should be getting better. As soon as I get home, I'll rub your back and footsies." He laughs and an announcement blares in the background. He's clearly in the hospital. "Where are you?"

I squeeze my eyes together and clench my teeth tight. *I hate lying.* "I'm at Fielding's. We're hanging out, watching TV." I hold my breath and feel its catch when I remember that I never turned on location services on my phone for him. "I do think I'm feeling better. I miss you, especially our morning time."

A woman's voice, not especially young, calls after him and he abruptly releases me from our call, but not before he tells me he loves me and can't wait to see me tonight. The line goes dead before I can reply, and I sit on the toilet for a while before I go back to the living room to hear Michelle's confessions. *You're being a total fucking dolt, Jenna. What liar calls and has that conversation? Have a mature discussion with him and clear this up the right way. Or, be a coward….*

"So, to treat myself for the engagement I went for a manicure, a blow out, and then a blow *job* with the single dad at work I've had the hots for…for like *forever*." Landi, Elizabeth, and Fielding are hanging on to Michelle's words—all for different reasons. "He's kinda quiet, maybe…probably a little lonely." She tilts her head up, her eyes starry and dilated. "We've talked a lot about work, about his kids and struggles trying to raise them pretty much alone. He seemed sad that day and I was so happy, so excited about the future. Dean had slipped the ring on my finger the night before, and I just slipped it off, tossed it in my desk drawer, then asked Mac to lunch—that's his name, Mac. He's not too tall, but well maintained—a little salt and pepper gray around the temples, the ribbed edge of his shirt, tight against his muscled biceps…a little swirly tattoo peeking out from underneath. I thought his waist would be cut, and I wasn't wrong. Lunch was exhilarating; I could have cut the tension with a plastic fork. My pussy was sopping wet even before I sealed the deal. He couldn't believe his luck; we talked, laughed, touched. He was starved for attention, now that I think about it. Perfect for plucking right up.

"I couldn't wait until we got back to his place. I loosened his belt, popped him right out of his pants, and went down with a vengeance on his hard cock, shoving it to the back of my throat because I knew, I *knew* he'd been waiting so long for that type of adoration, that type of cock worship I gave him. I nearly made Mr. Mac Daddy come right there in that parking lot, but we managed to get back to his apartment and collapsed on the bed in sixty-nine—my lips furiously worked him into my mouth. He was so, so hard, precum dripping down my open throat, my eyes wide and wet from his throbbing fullness sliding in and out of my mouth. Mac spun himself around and pinned me on the bed, biting my lip, teasing me with the head of his dick trying to pry my smooth pretty pink lips apart. He thought he was in control, so I said, 'I'll swallow your cock whole if you make love to my clit…take away my need for anyone else.' I knew good and well the anyone else part was the clincher. I wiggle out from under him and I take his full hard-on down to the top of his balls while his tongue double-flicks my clit until I come in his mouth with a guttural moan that's part pleasure, part pain, and part domination.

"And then he lost himself inside of my wetness—cursing and almost suffocating in his own desire to be known in a way he's never been known by a woman because I was officially 'off limits.' I'm his supervisor. I'm taken. I'm not right for him. He fell down that rabbit hole and I rescued him. Pulling out, he dropped his hot jizz all over my tits as I watched his face contort in passion and this realization: he's still got it. I made him remember that he was a man. And *that's* what will make me unforgettable to him."

"I'm pretty sure I'm gonna leave a wet spot on her couch," Fielding leans over and whispers to me.

My eyes twirl in all directions and Elizabeth is the only one who seems to be unaffected. Her lips stretched in her predictable smirk, eyes canvassing for anyone not under the spell of the Cheater's Club. Her eyes rest on me. *Me. Maybe we are more alike than I want to admit.* She claps and moves to the center of the room. "Well done, my dear. That was quite a celebration. Well done!"

Michelle's poised serpent tongue slowly licks some soy sauce off of her finger, and before she pops a piece of sushi in her mouth, she replies, "Well done, but not finished. There's more."

Elizabeth claps both her hands together in successive attempts to get Amanda's attention. "We'll need drinks refreshed and a new round of nibbles!" Elizabeth calls out in expectation that Amanda's service will be swift and utter perfection. "Don't make us wait, Michelle, darling. Whatever else did you do?" Elizabeth drapes herself across the back of the Italian leather couch, mocking the event with another martini.

"I go back to the office with the intent of finishing up a project, but as I'm walking in, Brents Lamb, owner of Scope Design, is walking out. Bastard's always trying to poach my people. Although we're work rivals, we've managed to keep a little flirty back-and-forth, made out a few times in the elevator at trade shows, but it never went any further than that. So, he tells me he wants to talk to me. I take him to my office and excuse myself to call Landy—my always-alibi who covers for me. Dean thinks she works with me, and Landy's husband thinks the same thing.

"When I return, he's got the blinds closed and my office door barely cracked. There's a box waiting for me on my desk, wrapped in a hot pink bow, and he's sitting in my chair, smiling like he's just eaten the ass-end out of something he shouldn't have. When I open the box, there's the most perfect dildo I've ever seen! Perfect length, width, it's soft and smooth.

"We both burst out laughing and he reminds me it will come in handy when I need a quick cure from all the headaches old married women are prone to getting. I look him straight in his eyes and ask, 'Is this what you look like?' His answer is unzipping his pants, and while he didn't quite match up to Mr. Big Dick, he didn't disappoint. My pussy is begging to be pounded—Brents or Mr. Big Dick, I don't give two shits. He puts himself in my mouth first and uses Mr. Big Dick to trace my lips, my jaw, down the small of my back, between my tits.

"Then I'm going back and forth between the two, getting them both all slobbery wet, and he grabs me by the arms and lifts me up, swiping the hem of my skirt to my waist, and pushes me stomach-first over the edge of my desk. Pulling my panties to the side, he puts Mr. Big Dick inside of me. I pull back on it like working a pump-action rifle, and the next thing I know, he stops me with a steady hand on my back and puts himself inside my ass. He's slow and methodical, the burn and stretching have me instinctively crawling up the desk away from him, but he grabs my shoulder and pulls back, not letting me get too far away.

"He takes the sample lube out of Mr. Big Dick's box and pours it all over himself until I can feel its cool relief and I relax, sucking him in most of the way. After four pumps his breathing is ragged and deep, and he comes in my ass while I quietly make a mess out of Mr. Big Dick. Then I put him—uh, Mr. Big Dick, that is—back in his box and shove him in my desk drawer. Brents hired my best drafter that next week—paid him almost double. Cocksucker."

Fielding is flushed from her cheeks to her chest and I wonder whether I should bury the cheese-serving knife in Michelle's head or have a totally inappropriate orgasm. For all its depravity, it's a hot story, and it makes me miss Collin even more, except that twinge of jealousy dampens my appetite for him—a little. Elizabeth dismisses everyone to the basement to check out the full renovation going on down there, just as if nothing happened. Fielding is frozen in her spot. She's kicked her heels off and let her legs helplessly splay open. "Fuck." That's her only word. For three minutes she says nothing else, and the two of us sit on the couch in our own wet puddles. "Should we go see the basement?" she asks.

"I think we probably should leave. Collin is supposed to be home soon and I'm feeling...."

"Worked up? Like you need another shower? Disgusted? Bad for Dean? All the above?"

"You forgot puking and squirting."

"Jenna, do you think we fit in here?"

A voice we'd forgotten about answers our question. "If you have to ask, then the answer is no. And be glad of it." Amanda offers us two sparkling waters and ushers us out the front door.

Chapter Six: A Perfect Illusion

The next week is a blur of work, children, and...worrying about Collin. It's not that he's unaffectionate, but *overly* affectionate and dutiful to my needs: foot rubs, back rubs, passionate sex, quality down time. I tell myself that I'm being paranoid, that I have nothing to worry about, and feeling more than a little guilty about asking for Elizabeth's help, if that's what it truly is. Sometimes, I hardly recognize myself anymore. And I don't like it. *Then make shit happen so that you do.*

As Collin cleans up the dinner dishes, I strike with my first question, "Are you happy?"

The wet plate in the sink drops and he answers my question with his own, "Why? Are *you* not happy?"

I look at him for a long while before I answer. As he dries his hands, I see him tear up a little. This is bothering him because in his universe, no good conversation begins with that question. "I feel...strangled. I think about our life together, what it could be, and...I'm not sure this baby is a good idea. It's just a lot, Collin, *a lot*."

His tears quickly turn to disgust and anger. "I thought we'd already discussed this. Now, you don't want this baby...with me?"

"Yes, well—no! No! That's not what I'm saying at all. Listen to me, I..."

"Oh, I am listening to you, and I can't believe you,

Jenna! I'm trying to give you the world—everything you want, everything you need, everything you didn't have in your first marriage. What the fuck? I'm working my ass off!"

"Are you cheating on me…or do you want to?" The words carelessly trip and tumble out of my mouth, knowing no time, no place, no limits except sweet relief that I've finally let the demon out of its cage.

Collin's face softens and he shakes his head. "Why would you think that?"

I dive my face into my hands as much out of embarrassment as shame for admitting my trespass. "I saw a note in your bag and—I snooped…the note from Lena. Who's Lena?"

Collin pinches himself between the eyes, that familiar move when he's trying not to come too fast, but this time, it's done in a move out of deliberate control of his words. "Lena is in my cadre, Jenna. It was an assignment. We're learning how to care for patients, how to be empathetic because sometimes doctors lose that, detach as a form of self-care. We were paired up…I did *not* pick her, and we had to do something nice for that person and have a personal conversation. I talked about *you*. I talked about *our* baby. I didn't do anything wrong. I *wouldn't* intentionally do anything wrong."

My gut adds *yet…*. "Sorry." I quickly remember Fielding's advice and add, "I guess the pregnancy…the hormones—I'm just feeling insecure, like all of this will be snatched away from me." I keep my face pasted to my palms because Elizabeth's *help* is too far in the works to stop, and I'm not even sure I should stop it.

"Don't you know I love you?" he asks, rounding the corner of the bar and wrapping me in his long, strong arms.

"Yes, I know that, but I also know that love and lust are two different things. Is she attractive?"

"Who?"

"Lena!"

"Well, yeah, I guess. Jenna, you know that attractive people come and go, but love is hard to find, *real* love, the kind of love that you build a life on. I'm not gonna throw that away for a cheap, meaningless lay. I mean, unless you want me to." He rolls his eyes. *He rolls his eyes.*

"Wow—just...wow. You think that's what I want? For you to fuck someone else?" I push away from him.

"I don't know, Jenna. It sure seems like you're trying to find an excuse *not* to be content with what we have. Or, am I just reading this whole thing wrong? Maybe I'm being *insensitive*?" He says the word with sarcasm, continuing to talk to himself.

Walking over to the dishwasher, he slams its door and wipes down the table with successive slaps of the paper towel. "I know I'm not saying the right things. I'm sorry. I'm exhausted. I'm stressed and I got mad— maybe I shouldn't have. I just thought you were as happy and as excited about our future as I am. You know, maybe you and Fielding can go on one of your girl trips? I think it might be good for you. Maybe it'll be good for us? It's hard to be a good partner right now, but I'm trying. I can't give you everything you need to be totally content...just go take some time for *you*, okay?"

I open my mouth to respond, but I can't think of anything to say, so I just nod my head in agreement. I want to tell him that I *am* happy...but I can't find the right words, the words to explain to him how our age difference might have finally caught up with us.

Collin lumbers over and scoops up my hands. "Let's just go to bed. Everything will be better after some good sleep."

And a good girls trip. We lie in bed, our backs touching, and I remember that he never answered my question.

***

Fielding watches me throw my things in a suitcase, trying to catch and fold as much as possible. "Happy days are here again, huh?"

"I talked to him last night."

"You did?" She grabs my arm and stops the launch of my still-warm curling iron into the suitcase. "So…it went well…enough?"

"I guess. We're both tired, irritable—for the same and different reasons. He said I seem to be working hard to be unhappy and that even though he loves me—"

"What?"

"He said 'I can't give you everything you need to be happy,' which is true. But the weirdest part is that he didn't *exactly* answer my question."

"Which was what?" She impatiently taps her foot and snatches my makeup bag out of my hand. "You can't pack worth a shit or tell a story. You know how OCD I am about packing."

"He loves me. He was annoyed that I didn't seem happy. He said she was just someone he worked with, the note was an assignment, and he has no interest in her. Although he did admit in a roundabout way she was attractive. He told me I needed some space, a girls trip with you."

"Well, if that isn't the kiss of kismet, I don't know

what is! Love isn't all titties and champagne, darling. You know that. And speaking of, did you pack some lingerie for the trip? The sex club said the dress code is smexy." She rubs her hands together, eyeing my tits. "The theme is Into a Dark Wonderland."

"I have a slutty black and purple Halloween outfit with lots of lace, but I doubt I can fit these in it anymore," I complain and point to my boobs.

"Nooo! That's *perfect!* Stuff it in a small bag because you can't wear it into the club. You have to change when you get there."

"Then what do I wear there? Are there changing rooms? A cover charge?"

"There, there, my naughty little knocked up sex kitten. I've taken care of everything. Just wear something kinda sexy—cocktail dress or something—don't worry if it's too tight or if your boobs hang out. Yes, there are private places to change and I bought a membership for both of us."

"A membership?! Like a membership to the wholesale grocery club? How often do you think we're going to go? How often do *you* plan to go?"

"I don't know—maybe a few times. It depends on how much I like it. You don't *have* to have sex. We can just go and have fun. It's a safe place; memberships keep out the riff-raff, and all the horny, handsy single guys. Oh! We can play with toys, too! Bring yours; I'm bringing 'Vader.'" A deep laugh escapes her throat. "We can pole dance, we can dance naked on tables if we want, we can explore our polyamorous sides, we can—"

"I don't fucking *want* to do any of that!" My voice echoes across the room and I cross my arms over my chest.

Fielding throws down the curling iron on the bed. "Damn, Jenna! You're officially no fun, as in *zero* fun. What the hell is wrong with you? Ever since you got pregnant, you've not been yourself. And I expected changes—I get it. But, you're a witch, and bitter, and boring. Lighten the fuck up and *live*. You're pregnant, not dead. You don't have to do anything you don't want to do—and that includes having this baby and marrying Collin."

Her words pommel me into an ugly-cry wreck. All the stamina I have to keep my proverbial shit together crumbles and I confess through sobs, "Sometimes I feel like two different people, like I'm not sure whether I should be responsible or frivolous. I want to be Collin's wife, but I don't want to lose myself. I have a responsibility to be a woman who doesn't exist in the morally gray shadows—"

"Oh good lord, Jenna! You *are* that woman! Being a good person doesn't mean you have to be *perfect*. You think you're the *only* person who suffers adult growing pains? Who says we have to have shit all figured out by a certain age? I'll say it again for the people in the back: You don't have to be fucking perfect! Just don't stop enjoying your own life. It seems to me that maybe Collin has a point: you're working pretty hard to make yourself miserable."

I put my still-blubbering head on her shoulder. "You know, Fielding, I kinda looked forward to turning forty—throttling life a little. I just didn't think I'd be trading one thrill ride for another."

"Honey, in this life, I don't think there's any other kind. Now, c'mon, we gotta get packed and go find the real Jenna."

****

Club Perceptions was nothing like I expected—but had everything I needed to change mine.

My new curves fill out my slutty, sexy little dress better than I had hoped. A cascade of my full breasts nearly spill out the top edges, and as I check myself out in the mirror, I notice a flock of eyes checking me out, too. It's not jealousy, as looks from other women can often be, but admiration…and even a hint of desire.

"You are ravishing! Holy shit! Look at *you!* Your boobs, your legs, your face and hair—you're literally glowing, Jenna!"

"You think?" I twirl like a ballerina, admiring myself again. And *loving* the newfound admirers.

"Yes, beeoch, I do think!" Fielding plies me with a full-body hug. "There's my confident, beautiful, feisty friend."

"You buy that special for tonight?" I point to the see-through chartreuse shirt and thong with black platform heels. I wind up my arm, smack her ass, until she jumps.

"Daaaamn! You practicing on your fuck boy or something?" She winks and firmly seizes my hand. "Let's go crazy!"

As Fielding and I leave the dressing room, we stroll past a shiny meadow of chrome stripper poles, women shimmying up and down them with a variety of skills. Some are hair-flipping, sensuous, highly sophisticated workers of the pole while others jump on and clumsily chafe themselves all the way down. Fielding spies an empty one near a back corner but is suddenly escorted away from the pole by Miss Member Services.

The club patrol is dressed in black denim chaps and

a suede vest, armed with a spray bottle and white towel. She gently escorts Fielding away from the pole then calmly yanks her back, whispering some sweet, devilish promise in her ear, smiling, then spraying and wiping the pole down until it glistens.

As I watch the muscles flex in Fielding's calves and biceps as she grinds and wraps her mile-high legs around the silver studs that stand at inexhaustible attention, I notice that *many* someones are watching. Her inhibition is gone—and we're both totally sober. We don't know anyone and they don't know us. We have everything and nothing to lose. We are young and old. We are lost and found. Tonight…we are free to be as fucked up as we want because tonight, we are finding out what makes us women who want the best life has to offer.

The bass riff is gruff and familiar, an intoxicating mix of forbidden pleasure and giving-no-fucks reluctance. Fielding curls her finger toward me, mouthing "Come here."

I reluctantly sashay over to her and take her outstretched hand. We grind on each other and on the pole, our sweat and juices dampening our panties, leaving steamy condensation marks on the pole. Our asses bump against two other women who are also grinding, and without thinking, without planning, I caress a plump ass cheek, not caring who it belongs to while a delicate, manicured hand stretches to cup my tit, ending with a full, firm squeeze. Tracing the edge of the brunette's hot pants, I slide my finger between her ass and pussy, rubbing it until we're both flushed with anticipation.

I look at Fielding over my shoulder and she's in an embrace with another woman who's set up shop behind

Fielding, grinding on her ass while wrenching Fielding's neck around to face her and plunging her electric pink tongue into Fielding's mouth. I watch as their soft lips smash together. *I'd love to have Collin's dick inside of me right now. Or any dick inside of me*, I add to myself, surprised I let myself consider the option.

I squeeze between Fielding and the redhead clutching her face, and yell above the music, "Let's go find a quiet place—toys!"

She reluctantly pulls away from the glistening skin of her playmate and we duck into the lockers to grab our dildos. Winding through the maze of half naked people, I remember I haven't thought about Collin tonight—and I don't want to. The strangers in this place, the strange things I don't normally do in front of strangers—everything makes me feel like I *belong*. No one here is themselves because we're all authentically responding to who *we* want to be—selfish, indulgent, sexual, perverse, flirty, friendly, human, and *normal*. As women, sometimes we're inadvertently sent mixed messages about how *not* to be sexual, except in certain situations with specific people. But if *everyone* is sexual, then why is that not acceptable to explore on *our* terms? Why is it labeled slutty when it should be applauded as genuine? Maybe it's because the Cheater's Club has been a good 'ole boy's club for too long.

Fielding and I order a couple mocktails and stroll through the couples and their guests slapped together like a messy PB & J. Mouths, hands, legs, tits, ass, and cocks are on display for show minus the tell. We find a corner with plush chairs and let our eyes roam the choices: The Saddle Room, Glory Hole Alley (with "cum cups"), The Confession Box, and Fantasy Rock. I peel the guide from between my sweaty tits and read about each one. "So, mutual masturbation is allowed in Glory Hole Alley and The Saddle Room, but not couples sex. That's only allowed in The Confession Box, which has a BDSM-theme and includes restraints and a bondage box, and Fantasy Rock, which has glow-in-the-dark hiding spots and features Sybian masturbation devices designed to look like monsters—reservations are recommended for those, though." Fielding snaps her fingers in disappointment. "Voyeurism is allowed in all spots except for the themed reserve rooms. Those are invitation-only."

"I feel like a kid in a fucking candy shop. Don't you? Don't you feel soooo fucking sexy…and *free*? I mean, where else can you watch people get tied up and spanked, or whack off in a random hole, or fuck some imaginary monster peen?"

"Hmmm…I once saw a woman luridly rub up against a grocery cart."

"Jenna, I'm glad you're *you* again. And for the record, I know things are hard…I get it, but you can be *you* even if you're a new wife and mommy."

"You must be hanging around smart people," I quip. "In honor of finding myself again, I want to see Glory Hole Alley. I'm kinda turned on by the scene. And you know what else?"

"You want to reserve a monster peen to ride?" Fielding asks, hunching her dildo.

"Well, yeah, but I was just thinking how much better this is than the Cheater's Club. You know?"

Fielding answers me by wagging her dildo in my face, breadcrumbing me, and I grab Vader like a sex-deranged Hansel and Gretel wannabe. "Come on, little girl...let's go watch the glory hole gang."

We walk hand-in-hand through a luscious concoction of sex—men, women, tits, hard cocks, curious fingers, moans, sighs, and air, briny-scented with the satisfaction of sex. Our baptism into Glory Hole Alley is a salt and pepper-haired shirtless man in Old West dusty brown chaps who gently guides his cock into a random hole in the wall while his couple—a woman sucking on his balls and a man entering his *own* glory hole from the back. We greedily watch as he's catching fuck vibes from all angles and settle on the love seat with our towels and toys. I'm afraid to touch myself at first, but the cowboy in the hole lassos my eyes and won't let go. His pleasure is complete, watching me watch him, the tip of my toy in my deliciously sopping wet hole, not giving two fucks who else is watching—until I see Fielding watching us.

"Stop! That's weird! You and I...no!"

"I'm sorry!" she offers, licking on Vader like a sucker. "It's hot! You and him...total strangers...and he's clearly very into you and...."

"Well endowed? And...uhm...fluid?"

"Maybe he's Cheater's Club worthy?" teases Fielding.

"Nah, I don't really think I'm designed that way—probably." But the thing is, I'm *curious*. I had imagined that post-divorce, I'd be free to fuck around and find out...at least for a little while. This man's ass, full of someone's else's cock and perfectly carved like a Halloween pumpkin, has got me wondering why being curious has to be a *calamity*.

I'm shaken from the voice in between my legs by a slap on the shoulder from Vader. "I'm going to go check out Fantasy Rock. I wanna ride a giant monster peen before we go…okay?"

"Sure! I'll be in the lounge area outside the dressing rooms. I'll wait." As I watch her skip out with Vader wagging back and forth in her tight fist, I feel another sort of clenching—salt n' pepper cowboy is done with his hole and wiping himself down, never taking his eyes off of me. His face drips with curiosity and a sly smile. *He knows I'm curious. He knows I'm a challenge, too. But am I completely off limits?*

He sidles up to me and without an invitation, settles himself beside me…*right* beside me. His muscular abs pop out, supporting him as he twists his chest toward mine. His eyes are light blue, almost steely gray, and a faded scar runs from his collarbone to his left shoulder. A crow tattoo flexes on his bicep as I nervously sit in my own juices, wondering what this man knows about me that I can't seem to figure out about myself.

"Hey. I'm Paul." He puts a fist toward mine for a pump. "It's cleaner that way. My kids have been sick and I've been hoping and praying I'm in the clear. A lil' germaphobey." He smiles and shrugs his shoulders, as vulnerable and honest as fuck. *Shit, shit, shit.*

He has kids…like me…and he's considerate, in shape, and clearly into experimenting. I'm acutely aware that minutes have passed as I'm lost in my own brain. "Oh! Yeah, I'm Jenna." I meet his fist with mine and blush with an awkward conveyance of attraction. "Uhm…sorry, this is my first time here. I don't know how all this works."

"You're great…you're doing great. You look like you belong. This is just my third time, my second with my friends." He points to the couple walking toward the

84

private rooms. "I'm here with them. Single guys can't just walk in. I guess they think they can't trust us around so many ravishing women. Of course, some are so much more ravishing than others." He smiles again and locks me dead on with his fuck-me bedroom eyes. *Shit, shit, shit—again!*

I awkwardly change the subject. "Am I allowed to ask you where you're from and what you do?"

He scoots his ass closer to mine and I steal a glance at his package—it's swollen and fills up the cup of his thong, his balls nearly spilling over the edges. I know he catches me because when I try to meet his eyes I discover that he's playing hardball—he's visually motorboating my tits like he's on vacation at the lake. His shrug and deliberate return to my tits delivers a one-two sucker punch realization: *I could be his and no one would ever have to know. Except...I'd know. The hardest person to disappoint is yourself.*

"I'm from Nashville originally, but I live in Franklin now. I work in IT and I have twins—two boys. They're thirteen going on thirty. What else, Jenna? What else do you want to know because I know you want to know, right?" He hovers close enough to my ear that I can feel his hot breath and I wince as he licks my ear lobe.

A flurry of panic rises in me that matches my desire. *Run.* "I'm sorry," I stammer, "I didn't come here for, for this—I need to leave." I let my hand graze close to his crotch.

A wave of disappointment paints his face crimson and apologizing, he adds, "I get it. Maybe this is just a story for the 'ole deathbed, huh? But if you ever change your mind...here's my card. You're stunning, and I like your vibe, which is not something I find that I can say a lot. I've never been able to define what *it* is, but I know you've got it." As he gets up and walks away, I watch his ass flex in his chaps and wonder what the hell just happened…and regretting (just a little) what *didn't* happen.

I bashfully stumble over the foot of a table toward the dressing rooms while my eyes fill with tears. *You've got it.* I can only surmise that the reason fate intervened and made it possible for me to go with Fielding has very little to do with sex and the brain between my legs, and everything to do with that little nagging voice in my brain that is trying to calculate my heart's happiness one decision at a time. I almost throw Paul's card in the garbage can, but fold it and decide to stick it between my boobs for safe keeping because I suddenly remember Lena's note to Collin. *Cheaters get karma.*

"Am I being a bad influence?"

I turn toward the familiar voice and grab Fielding's hand, pulling her into a changing room. "We need to get the hell out of here…now!"

"Did something happen?" I yank off my sexy lingerie as Fielding continues to yap at me while I pull on my travel outfit. "Because if he did something, I'll put a boot up his sexy ass," she growls.

"No, nothing happened, but if I stay any longer I won't be able to say that. C'mon, Fielding! Get outta the hoochie momma outfit and let's leave before my pussy declares mutiny!" As I hopefully watch the floor for Paul, waiting on Fielding, I remember. "So, how was the monster peen?"

"Uh, it was okay—a dressed up dildo that I boinked with some scary shit on the walls and scarier people watching. That part was kinda fucking awesome. I felt bad, though—cheated on Vader."

"I'm sure he'll understand." I roll my eyes, standing guard while she strips down.

"Are you sure you don't want to stay? Find out what you're missing?"

"You know what? You're *totally* a bad influence. I hope you get a monster peen venereal disease."

Her laugh turns sincere. "It's tempting though, isn't it?"

"Nah. My panties are just swimming-pool wet because I'm excited about the cookie I'll find on my pillow before bed at our cheap-ass hotel. Why the hell do you think I'm needing to leave...like yesterday? And what about you? No one for you who's club worthy? Lots of hot guys...and girls."

"Meh...Maybe I need more than something physical. I suppose when I know I'll know, but—not tonight."

"Next week is your week to share," I remind her. "You can't say that."

"That's why I have *you*. We'll have to muck together a story from tonight—monster peen, glory holes, stripper poles. No one will ever know—a handful of truths and a few lies."

"No one will ever know, and that includes Elizabeth." A devious smile Elizabeth would be proud of crowns my face. "'Engineering an outcome...destruction optional' as she says."

Fielding's only response is this: "Cheers to the Cheater's Club." She shoots back the rest of her drink and hands me the keys.

Chapter Seven: Love, Lies, and Complications

It's the end of week ten.

My guilty conscience cuts me some slack and my head falls to the pillow Monday night after my Nashville weekend. I only feel like a shitty human when Collin asks me what Fielding and I did. I don't tell the *whole* truth, but I do tell the *other* things we actually did like shopping at some outlets, seeing a couple impromptu live music gigs, people watching on Broadway, and checking out a few restaurants plus the Parthenon. The rest of the truth wouldn't be useful to him, and it's a double-edged dagger I'm tasked with hiding. *How can I want and expect him to be honest when I so easily lie...and for what?* For what...that's the answer to the question that swirls and goes stale in my brain. My whole life I've played fair. I've done the right thing. Other people's feelings have come before my own. I've sacrificed, been content with less than my personal best for the sake of another person's ego, and damn...I'm exhausted. *What does that have to do with being a liar?* To be a liar is to preserve a piece of yourself behind an invisible smokescreen—and if you're lucky, no one else finds out about it. And if you're *really* lucky, you'll parlay that shit into a life that you want—collateral damage be damned. While no one particularly likes a liar, liars might just have the upper hand because they don't worry about anything except what they owe *themselves.* It might taste like shit going down, but I'm ready with my glass of poison.

"I missed you, you know that? In less than six months you'll be my wife...my wife!" Collin squeals and his voice breaks.

"I missed you, too." It's an automatic reply that I know doesn't have a lot of passion behind it. It's not that I *haven't* missed him, but that I've really enjoyed getting back to my old self again, which is a relationship no one can afford to sacrifice. "That's crazy! It doesn't seem like it should be here already." I don't want to give away that I'm not interested in talking about the wedding, so I change the subject. "How was the week? Better than before?"

"Oh, absolutely! I feel like I've hit my groove and Luke and I are vibing on the same page in the cohort. We started seeing patients this week."

"Oh? Luke? That's a new name."

"Nah, Luke's been there since the beginning, but got moved into my cohort. He and I are specializing in the same thing, and we just have similar personalities, backgrounds. It's been cool to have a new friend to kick around with during breaks."

"What happened to Lena?" I ask, after turning over and spooning my backside into him.

Collin nuzzles his nose in my hair and reassures me. "You don't need to feel threatened by Lena, okay? Besides, she moved to a new cohort. Her specialty is pediatric oncology. You're the one I adore, Jenna. Don't you know that?"

I spin back to face him and ply him with a wet kiss that ends with my tongue circling his lips. "You better" is my only response. I reach down between his legs to find that his length and girth have swelled to their impressive proportions and my juices quickly fill my hole that anticipates his cock slowly sliding deep inside that wet mound of fuck juice I've prepared…just for him.

Heat rises between us as our tongues move in and out. With his hard dick in my one hand and his balls in another, I wrap my top leg over his and grind into him. "Take me, fuck me so slow until I almost come," I whisper, squeezing my handful of balls.

He obeys with an obedient groan, his own slick juice running from the head of his dick mixing with mine for the perfect combustion. His pump is methodical, retarded only by my instructions, and I've collapsed around his shaft for the perfect fit of satisfaction tinged with the slightest of discomfort. Collin plunges in and out, but only removing himself barely. He kneads my tits with his hands, enjoying their fullness. He vigorously licks my big nipples, all the while attesting with a loud grunting satisfaction.

"I can feel that tight pussy. Does my beautiful momma wanna come? If she does, she better beg for it, 'cause I need to know you're worth it."

I bury my teeth in the flesh of his shoulder and whisper, "Please…I'm so fucking worth it!" I hiss, the familiar wind up falling fast. "When I come, I'll suck you in so deep you'll never be able to escape. You'll wanna walk around forever with me swinging on the end of your dick."

"Ah, ah, ah! That doesn't sound like begging. That sounds like a threat." He squeezes my nipples until I yelp—a cascade of yelps and guttural moans of fantastic vibrations—immediately blasting me into the perfect orgasm. I clench my walls around his cock; I can't stop the juicy rippling up and down his shaft. "I guess there just wasn't time for too much begging, huh?" he whispers, beginning the deepest part of his fucking. With every stroke I watch his face cloud with a selfish want of one thing.

"Fuck my tight little pussy like you want to hurt it! Fuck me! Show me who's the best at filling my holes," I command. As the head of his cock expands, his breathing is strenuous and he lets a profanity-laced train of compliments slide into my ear with the tip of his tongue tracing my lobe, designed with one end in mind: my pleasure. "You make me come so hard I forgot your name!" I giggle in his ear.

"You better *never* forget *my* name," he growls, seizing my throat until I can feel my pulse throbbing under his thumb. "'Cause I'll never forget yours, Mrs. English."

Collin kisses me until I forget whose air I'm breathing and I rake my nails down his clenched fingers. His hips slap into me and I dig my fingertips into his ass, exploring his crack as far as I can reach, as far as he'll let me. Images of Paul flash in my mind and I can hear Collin moaning as his dick swims in my fuck juice. I wriggle and then dip my pinky to my crotch for lube. I carefully trace his ass with my pinky until I feel him relax and coax me to go deeper.

His pumping slows until my pinky catches his rhythm and I take his hand, wanting more than one hole filled. "Don't leave out my hole," I cooly whisper in his ear. He traces my wet spots and as I feel him harden inside of me, the tip of his pinky sinks into my ass. A sweet heat singes my insides and scents the air, spilling across my body, reverberating with our double chorus of fuck yeahs as we both reach the pinnacle of satisfaction.

We lie in bed spooning, listening to the birds coo as they roost. I'm almost asleep when Collin sighs deeply in relaxation, only to nervously clear his throat. "Babe, do you really want to get married?"

He can read my mind. It's the question I've been afraid of asking him, and even afraid of considering myself. I don't want to lose Collin, but if I marry him…*will I lose myself?* "Why? Do you not want to get married?"

His grip tightens around me and he answers to the back of my head. "I do want to get married, and I want to marry you, but I was thinking after our conversation the other day that…maybe you need more time, which is okay. I think maybe I've been selfish; I've forgotten you're not in the same place I am, and that the changes to our lives are totally hitting you differently."

I want to turn to face him, but I can't. And not because I can't be honest, but because seemingly innocent conversations like these often produce a glaring honesty that leads to painful realizations. I gulp and confess, "I love you, but…."

"There's a but," he says. "That's never good."

"No, it's not that! I just need time. I know what I want, but I'm not sure I'm ready for it right now, Collin. I feel like I'm in a pressure cooker." Even in the dark I can see the tears welling in his eyes. His silence is eerie and I wonder whether we're pulling away or pushing closer.

"Jenna…if you don't want to get married, please just tell me. I know I want to spend the rest of my life with you. Do you know that? Because if you don't, then—."

I carefully spin my body to face his. "Of course I do!

You know how much I love you, but timing can be a bitch. I don't want things to change between us," I stutter, confusion circles my brain. "Can we just live together for a little while longer? Put the wedding on hold and just…be together?"

"Yeah! Absolutely! Jenna, I just want to be with you. I never want you to feel trapped, to feel like you can't talk to me, or that I'm unsupportive. We can wait. I'd wait forever for you. The only thing I can't do is let you go. That's how much I love you, babe. I'll love you—even if you don't feel the same."

"But I do," I whisper as he collapses his arms around my body and rocks me back and forth in bed. A relief I've not known in several weeks covers me. The idea of marriage has been too confining; it's not the idea of being monogamous or in an exclusive relationship with Collin. *Are promises and commitments only good on paper?* I think the Cheater's Club proves that's a dangerous assumption.

As I roll back over to face the wall, he is hesitant to let me lie free from his arms and he scrunches closer to me. His hands snake to my breasts and gingerly roll them between his hands. I sigh, "Don't you ever get enough? I can't keep up."

Collin laughs. "I just like this—me and you. I want you to be happy, and I hope this makes you happy— satisfied. I want to make your life better, not more complicated. Hmmm…" he adds, sitting up a little in bed.

"What's wrong? What is it?" He pushes more into my breast with his index and middle fingers. "Collin? What're you doing?"

"Ah…I thought I felt something."

"Something like my boob?" I snort.

He reaches behind him and taps the light on, examining the skin on my right breast. "It's probably nothing." He stretches his head, examining the skin.

"What's nothing?"

"I felt a lump, but it's likely just a milk duct, or maybe even a cyst. Just mention it to the doctor the next time you go for a check-up, which is when, by the way? I think I'd like to start going with you if I can swing it in my schedule."

"It's in a couple weeks. You think everything is okay?"

He reaches over and turns the light off. "I'm not worried about it at all. Get some sleep. I love you, Jenna." A dozy kiss lands on my cheek.

As my heart beats a lonely solo in my ears, I listen to Collin's breath ripple to a measured snore as he drifts off to sleep. *A lump. So much for not making my life complicated.*

Chapter Eight: Where the Wild Things Go

I'm in no mood for cute cucumber canapés, and certainly can't enjoy the mojitos, so I make an executive decision to snoop in Elizabeth's house. Her walk-in closet is the same size as Jacob's bedroom and her bathroom would put the local spa to shame. I rifle through her drawers for unmentionables. *Anything I can use against her.*

In the middle of her walk-in closet I find a small multi-story jewelry box full of sparkling rings and bracelets. *These must be the 'I'm guilty, please don't take half' bobbles.* I suspect it won't be an easy ask...requesting that she stop my Cheater's Club investigation into Collin. Besides the dirty jewelry, I only find expensive clothes, expensive makeup, decadent tastes—all with a price tag that I can hardly stomach: she and her husband take turns sitting on the liar's throne, which doesn't bother me as much as the fact that they only pretend to thrive on jaded love and dubious intentions.

I spin on my heels and look for something to spit on—*total heathen—her, not me.* My parched-mouth spittle lands on Elizabeth's monogrammed silk pillow. A roar of wicked, lilting laughter draws me downstairs where I find Fielding stalling until she senses me at her side.

"There she is, one of the women of the hour. Did

you get lost?" Elizabeth's words fail to thrash my confidence. "I hope you found what you were looking for."

"I was looking to satiate my appetite for destruction. I guess I'll have to look somewhere else for that."

"I have a feeling that you'll find it soon," Elizabeth teases. "I think what you'll get exactly what the doctor ordered." She winks and turns away from me. "This week is our special two-for-one. It's Landy's turn for an update and Fielding Giles' week to share for the first time, and I absolutely cannot wait for her first report to the Cheater's Club." Elizabeth clamps two veiny hands over Landy's shoulders, nudging her forward.

Dressed in a flesh pink cap-sleeved blouse and black fitted skirt, Landy's long, tanned legs in black patent leather heels tap at us like chum in the water. We're all frenzied, nearly fried to our wits end with want. Landy is brilliant, brazen, in possession of a million-dollar mind a lot of us would kill for, and a heart made for bad, bad intentions. No one here should enjoy this as much as we do, but…we do. *Damn, we so do.*

"My research assistant this past semester was the best…uh…in so many senses of the word," she gushes, blushing at a hidden memory we're hoping she'll share. "He and I…we're on the same wavelength and he's a marvelous researcher, just the epitome of dedication. I don't know that I would have finished my book and got it off to press without his help." She bashfully bites her lower lip, adding, "Of course, *I* wouldn't have gotten off without his help in that department, too."

"Darling," Elizabeth intrudes, "just give us the dirty details. At the rate you're going, the mint in the mojitos will wilt. Move it along." She impatiently turns her hands in a circular motion.

"Vaughan was so much more to me than a brain. We loved connecting…especially in the library. I may have been a nerd in college, but I learned my lessons in the library. We're on the fourth floor, or what I like to call 'four on the fourth floor.'" Landy giggles too long at her own pun, her nude lip gloss catching the light refraction in her glass, throwing jealous daggers as her stage lights.

"He texted me and asked that I meet him there at two o'clock—*sans* panties, a long jacket, glasses, and heels—nothing else. Old books, unlike old men, turn me on, so I had made enough fresh cream on my way across campus to be sentient of the fact that we needed to be quick and intentional because the fourth floor can be a popular place, especially if anyone should see me in my library getup. I'm nearly taken by an involuntary orgasm when I clock Vaughan in my sights: five o'clock shadow, sandy blond hair flipped and neatly parted to one side, a baby blue oxford shirt unbuttoned, the tops of his pecs puffed up, his rich brown eyes looking like they want to dunk me, fold me. And those lips…pinched pink harboring the whitest teeth. He tugs me toward the back of the tall stacks and his friend Lief is there, who is a hazelnut blond version of Vaughan, less about twenty IQ points…but he more than made up for it with his cock." She balls up her hand and juts it out in front of us. Fielding moans and quietly stomps her feet.

"Vaughan kneels in front of me, licking my pussy, while Lief takes his taste from behind. As they peel my jacket off of my shoulders, they unzip, their pants hanging off their hips. I go to grab their cocks and discover that Lief has two—he's diaphallic! Do you know how genetically rare that is? That was Vaughan's little gift to me. He knows how much I'm aroused by genetic abnormalities."

We've all surely given ourselves concussions from all the involuntary slapping of hands across heads. Two cocks. One man. I have no words, but fortunately other people do.

"You had not one, not two, but *three* hard penises at your disposal?" Fielding groans.

"You totally deserve it...bitch!" Michelle mews from the kitchen. "I'm gonna need his digits."

Elizabeth stiffly clears her throat, her polite way of getting Landy back on track.

"The only thing I want to do more than study it is shove it in my mouth. But I want to see the boys cross swords, watching their precum catch the fine book dust floating in the air. Vaughan pushes me down—doesn't ask. I take turns deep throating each one, Lief's especially hard to handle and it takes some cock canoodling to make it work as neither thing one nor thing two are particularly small. I ask Lief, 'Can I get an order for each hole?'

"'No, but I can give you a double, if you'd like, ma'am.'

"Leaning against Vaughan, he helps me prop my legs on the table and spread my lips open. Lief produces a little bottle of his homemade lube—he's a chemistry adjunct, so I *totally* trust him—and he gently glides into me. The burning and stretching are intense at first, and I almost scream, except Vaughan has a free hand, which clamps tightly over my mouth. 'Aaaah! Just relax, doctor, let Lief do his experiment. What's research without a little hard work and torture?' he says.

"Lief doubles down, sliding deeper, faster. His

ragged hazelnut bangs are caught in the sweat of his flushed face; a bead of sweat drips off his nose. My pussy is making cream again...this is the worst work I've done in the library and I'm so proud of it!

"I bite Vaughan's finger and he jerks my head back, shoving his tongue in my mouth. He stops eating my face and moves over my body to start on my clit; he's watching Lief. Vaughan rolls back over my face and unzips his pants while I suck his balls and he strokes himself. I'm watching him watch Lief.

"The sensation—ecstasy in pain, my third eye blind knows the gents are getting off as much on their chemistry, no pun intended, as they are from my body, and the knowledge that I'm probably one of a few women who've had this opportunity—it gets me so hot my pussy is about to blow steam. The rush of contractions forces my ass to buck off the table and then the most astonishing thing happens...Lief comes—not out of just one dick, but *both* of his dicks and Vaughan follows suit almost immediately, coming all over my chin, tits, and even on Lief's dick. It was the most arousing, beautiful orgasm I've ever seen, like a waterfall, a fucking perfect oasis of come.

"I don't think the fourth floor will ever be the same." Landy breathes out a long sigh and the temperature in the room is about 102 degrees. No one speaks. No one knows what to say until Elizabeth announces a break, and snaps at Amanda for fresh drinks, then turns on Fielding. commanding her to ready her performance.

Fielding stammers a little as she gets going. "Damn, girls, that's a hell of a story to follow."

I keep time with Elizabeth's steady state of suspicion toward me. I nudge Fielding and wink at her, which I don't try to hide from Elizabeth. I add, "You ladies will want to take notes. This smoke show, like the last one, has a story with a little something for everyone," I tease, although I agree with Fielding that following up a story with two men and three penises is going to be a challenge.

"This past weekend, Jenna and I went to a sex club in Nashville. There were definitely some check marks earned for the bucket list," she teases. Glassy-eyed and glistening, I replay our adventure as Fielding weaves the actual events of the night with her voyeur edits. Michelle nearly sucks a chunk of feta down her throat when Fielding, with a twinkle in her eyes, casts herself as Paul's glory hole assistant, detailing every inch of her ball-sucking skills. Her monster-peen finale, with full-on heavy description of the two-headed monster junk designed to push a mortal woman to her limits, delivers us all to a sizzling mental climax.

Over the howls and the claps, we hear a phone ringing, which Elizabeth quickly seizes as an opportunity to chide us all about discretion. Landy tightly hugs her cell to her body and scurries to the powder room down the hall. Elizabeth is conspicuous, checking her watch for messages and ferrying water and headache medicine back and forth to the powder room while initiating the kind of eye contact with Shelby Lee that can only mean one thing: the shit's hit the fan for someone.

I lean into Fielding's space and whisper, "What the hell do you think that's all about?"

"I don't know," she mumbles, in between stuffing a canapé into her mouth, "but I'd say we're not going to find out anytime soon."

Shelby Lee emerges from the hall flushed and visibly upset. Fielding and I ferry ourselves toward her as she turns to face Amanda in the kitchen.

"Shelby Lee!" I whisper. "Is everything okay? It seems like there's something going on between Landy and Elizabeth."

Shelby Lee reluctantly spins on her heels, biting the bottom of her lip. "Uhm…I'm not sure," she lies, a hangdog shade eclipsing her face. Her head swivels side to side. "I shouldn't tell…Elizabeth told me not to tell, but Landy needs a friend. She doesn't need Elizabeth getting involved any more than she already is."

Fielding pipes in, "Elizabeth said we shouldn't have secrets, remember? She said this is a safe place." I'm not sure that's *exactly* what Elizabeth said, or even what she meant, but I'm going with it because clearly this is a matter of importance to Shelby Lee, and therefore, to us because Landy isn't the only one who needs a *true* friend. Not the kind like Elizabeth who'd lance you like a boil if she had even half a good reason.

With her lip sticking out and trembling, she parses out her words. "Landy is a professor. She has to publish to keep her job. The research—she did with her *much* younger research assistant. And that was a whole other story for the Cheater's Club files. Anyway, she joked around that they might have made up a source or two. We laughed it off. Landy is brilliant. She'd never do that…or at least that's what I thought. Turns out…that book she published to critical acclaim in the academic community? *Many* manufactured sources."

Fielding's teeth chatter and nearly drop out of her mouth. "She made up sources? Are you fucking kidding me? My husband's a professor and that's probably the *one* thing that could actually get you fired in academia. Man, talk about the road to deep shit! No wonder she's a basket case."

"What's she going to do?" I ask.

Shelby Lee hunches her shoulders to her ears and gently replies, "I guess go and beg for mercy to her dean, her publisher. I mean, I don't know what else she could do? Her research assistant is long gone. I wonder if she'll throw him under the bus?"

"How did the dean find out?" Fielding questions. I notice that Amanda is close to us—too close—and I get the impression that she's trying to listen to our conversation.

"An anonymous call…someone who knew a lot about it—a fellow researcher who loves to check out newbies, maybe? Landy's put Elizabeth on it. That bitch knows everyone, and there's no one who doesn't owe her something. It's uncanny. She will ferret out the rat and…I hate to imagine what that person's fate will be."

I think about the request I made to Elizabeth and wonder if it's too late to call it off? A glass shatters on the ceramic tile floor behind me. An alarmed Amanda is frozen with her hand to her mouth as Elizabeth rounds the corner at the commotion.

"Well, clean it up! Don't just stand there because I can pay *anyone* to just stand there and look shocked," she hisses.

Feeling brazen and insulated from Elizabeth's wrath by Landy's circumstances, I ask, "May I speak to you? I need to have a moment alone with you."

She whirls around, her straight-edged bob swinging around with her. I summon as much courage as I can. "Elizabeth, I'm no longer in need of your services. I don't need the Cheater's Club to check up on Collin. I appreciate—"

"You don't just call off my services, Jenna! People and placements are in motion."

"Well—things are good now. I was having a pregnant pause, so to speak, and I—"

"What? You thought you'd just make a request I couldn't resist and then…rudely rescind? Leaving me without anything to do?"

"This isn't a game, Elizabeth! This is me, my kids, Collin—real people!" The tone and volume of my voice is enough to get some heads to suddenly swivel like hyenas at a fresh kill.

"Oh, my dear, life is no more than a game. How could I stop for a moral consideration? If nothing else, don't you want to know the limits of the man you're going to marry, the father of your child? And most importantly, don't you want to know *yours*?"

"I know mine! *And* I know his. I don't need to *test* him. *Please,* Elizabeth!"

"Oh! Begging is attractive on no one! Come with me. I have something to show you."

I follow Elizabeth to a small office behind the walk-in pantry. The thick wood-grained door has no knob; she pushes on a particular edge of the door and it springs back, then opens. It's her office…the place where she surely makes mayhem for foolish people…people like me.

From her chrome-trimmed white leather chair, Elizabeth slaps a manila folder across the polished blond oak desk. It has my initials at the top—J.C.

"Go ahead…your guessing game is strong?"

I don't answer her because what I want and what I

anticipate could have two different outcomes, and the surprising thing to me is that I'm not exactly sure which one I want. *I'm indifferent.* With damp hands, I slide the envelope toward me and open it. Black and white photos of Collin and a young, attractive woman having lunch, obviously on different days. In one photo he's sitting on the same side of the table as she, and one photo has him hugging her beside his car. I recognize his dress shirt in one photo—it's from the day of our kitchen conversation, the one that made me feel relieved. *Now maybe I know why he didn't answer me directly when I asked him if he was cheating.* The minutes eek out an awareness that Elizabeth is not only watching, but calculating—calculating my next move so that she can plan her own.

A giant lump in my throat nearly stifles my response. "These don't prove an affair, necessarily. "

"True. Lunching doesn't *necessarily* lead to hunching. But, it's been my experience that it's a good start. Surely, you're not so daft that you'd do anything except agree with that, yes?"

As I stand with the pictures in my hand, I tear them into strips, scattering her desk with them. "You know, I'd put a lot more confidence in your skills if you weren't the kind of bitch who seemed to enjoy other people's pain so much."

Walking out, she reminds me of one reason that the Cheater's Club exists: "Better your pain than mine."

With tear-blurry eyes, I quickly try to cut through the kitchen to Fielding when something yanks at my arm.

"Don't let her hook you like this, into thinking that the only way to deal with a less-than-perfect life is to make someone else more miserable." Amanda's bold green eyes meet mine. "Her whole goal is to destroy the one thing she's never had—love. And my goal is to stop her in any way I can. I can help you, if you'll help me." Amanda scurries back to the sink as Elizabeth slithers from the wall, unaware of the snake in her own garden.

Chapter Nine: The Best Last Secret

I'm glad Fielding is keeping it a surprise who we're meeting for lunch because otherwise I would have dug my heels in and refused. I guess I'm a little heartless because the more I think about Collin's possible affair, the more I think that it might not be a totally awful thing. Get it out of his system. Then focus on being the man and father I need. I want. I deserve. *But what do you do with that betrayal?* You can walk away from physical intimacy with someone. *Smash n' pass.* I get that…wanting to fuck someone else. I get needing a refresher, a change of pace, a change of headspace, even. Hell, I can even understand an accidental, feral hard-dick-wet-pussy-oh-shit-here-we-go-moment. But what about having a connection and a shared space with someone? *Liking* someone? There's no betrayal like the betrayal of a friendship, which is where most meaningful relationships should at least start. That hurts. That's shattering. That's all the justification I need for…revenge. And when you start thinking like that, sometimes it's the beginning of the end.

"So, what's up? What's the mystery?" I snarl, impatient for the waiting—and the food.

"Oh, hi Jenna! How are you? Well, I'm fine. How are you, Fielding? Geez…what's crawled up your ass? Need more Nashville?" Fielding smirks, and I'm not amused.

"Elizabeth gave me pictures of Collin hugging Lena and he found a lump in my breast, which is probably nothing, but…what the fuck. Like I need something else to worry about?"

"Shit. I don't think they'll let us sit here long enough or we'll be able to order enough to solve this. I knew I should have picked an all-you-can-eat buffet," she snickers.

"Fuck you, Fielding!" It was louder, more pronounced than I had intended.

She reaches across the table and snatches my hands. "Stop! This isn't us. Did you ask Elizabeth to call it off?"

"Yes," I answer, my voice is wobbly. "But she refused. She said things are in motion, and…she likes messing with people's lives, especially mine."

"And have you talked to your doctor? You know lumps and shit in your titties are par for the course during pregnancy. Don't worry until you have something to worry about, but I get it, Jenna. You're fucking neurotic these days…and wearing me out."

I heave her hands up and cup them around my face. "I'm sorry. I know…I'm wearing myself out." My voice breaks and rises to a high pitch at the end.

"I think our lunch date today may help us shut Elizabeth down once and for all—at least one of your problems will be solved. And I have an electric knife…if you need my skills."

"Boobs and Collin's dick?"

"Two for one, babe. Love you."

"Hey girls! Thanks for meeting me." A voice with a subtle country twang sings to us.

Shelby Lee's feathery copper curls prance back and forth as she takes her seat. Her eyes sparkle with the joyful despair of a woman who's accepted that in the ruins of life, she's found her phoenix. Motioning toward Fielding, she asks, "You tell her my plan?"

Fielding shakes her head and I feel like the odd man out. "What kind of plan?" I ask.

Shelby Lee motions to the waitress while she explains. "Johnny is close. The doctor said major organs are beginning to shut down; he might have a couple, three weeks. Chris and I have talked about it—and we talked about it with Johnny. When Johnny dies, I'm leaving with Chris. We're getting out of here. I can do hair anywhere. He can be a hospice nurse anywhere. It's time for a fresh start, but I have something to do before I leave."

Confused, I shake my head. "What do you mean? Just leave! Why can't you just leave?"

"When I was recruited by Elizabeth, everything in my life was spinning out of control. My mom was out of work and living with us and my marriage...we were having issues like a lot of couples do. Johnny and I talked about separating, but then he was diagnosed and deteriorated quickly. I can't really tell you exactly what I was thinking, but the idea of being free appealed to me. Elizabeth was a client at the time and she encouraged me—in a good way—until I let down my guard and started joking around about how hot Johnny's hospice nurse was. I had no intention...and I felt terrible about maybe being a little relieved at Johnny's diagnosis.

"For the first time since I was in my twenties, I felt...unchained. Elizabeth suggested I talk to Chris about it. He assured me it was all normal, and he was professional about it. No come ons, no awkward forward moves. It was all me. I did it. And Elizabeth cheered me on, helped me justify it in the nicest way…until I realized why: She wanted a pain project, someone whose life was even more of the proverbial shit show than hers.

"And if she had to make it happen, all the better. I only found out after the fact that Elizabeth had visited Johnny in the hospital, when he was in treatment. I'm not exactly sure what she told him, but the way he looked at me that evening when I visited…I knew she'd told him *something*. Elizabeth threatened me; she said if I didn't join the Cheater's Club, she'd give Johnny pictures and 'enough details to kill him.' Her exact words. By the end of that week, he slipped into a coma and has been in one since.

"So, Chris and I decided to tell Johnny, and I feel like maybe…maybe now I have his blessing. Maybe he understands. So, while I *could* just simply leave, I won't unless I can finally give Elizabeth what she deserves."

Fielding slumps over the table with her head in her hands, chiming in, "Talk about sympathy for the devil. She's a sociopath…a *pathetic* sociopath. I can't believe I'm part of this."

With the wheels in my mind turning, I ask, "Were you the one who ratted out Landy?"

"No, but I know who did…and why. And Michelle is next."

Fielding and I exchange looks, without an inkling of truth between us about the person responsible for likely ruining Landy's career. And Michelle's life, too. We both sit patiently, waiting for her confession, which doesn't immediately materialize.

"I…it's hard to know who to trust. There's been so much deceit," Shelby Lee stammers.

"You can trust us," I offer. "We want to

help…without destroying anyone except maybe Elizabeth."

"Seems like we're all on the same page: Let's save our best last fuck for the Cheater's Club," Fielding offers with a heavy karate chop to the table.

"The only thing is this: You can't shatter Elizabeth without breaking her muse."

"Huh?" Fielding's eyes canvass Shelby Lee with suspicion and confusion. "You mean this person is her foil *and* her inspiration? Who the hell could that possibly be?"

Shelby Lee takes a long slurp of iced tea through her straw and answers. "Amanda."

Chapter Ten: The Hunting Kind of Happy

"I'm on my way, babe. Your appointment is for 10:45, right?"

I confirm and end the call with Collin, throwing my cell in the passenger seat. Sitting in the cool shade of the parking garage, I'm half tempted to skip the appointment. Hearing the baby's heartbeat, seeing its little body swim inside of me—I should be happy, even overjoyed, counting my blessings that both of us have been healthy so far, but there's this nagging doubt that binds me in a sorrow I can't shake. *What if this is a hunting type of happy?* The kind of happy that comes with singed edges and holes that I wonder whether can be mended—hunting hard for those silver linings. *Is happiness like that even considered a blessing?* I gulp hard, blinking back tears when a rap at my window nearly jolts my bladder into a quick release. *Collin.*

"What are you doing? C'mon! I don't want to be late," he yells through the glass.

I wipe my eyes as I pretend to pick something up off the passenger floorboard. "What? Don't you want to practice making people wait on you? Isn't that part of learning to be a doctor?" I grin, feeling pretty plucky at the realization that maybe this appointment is going to suck as much as my attitude. *Good. Bring it on...fate is a bitch? I'm way worse today.*

The elevator doors easily slide open as we

approach—no waiting. No one at check-in or in the lobby. Fast and efficient. A quick ultrasound—the baby is perfect and my breast…dense *(like my head)* and most likely a cyst, which is common during pregnancy. I precariously inhale the collective relief of my OB and Collin, who, by the way, crosses paths with his radiologist intern friend who does us a favor—he'll get the results read, maybe tonight. There's no line at The Smokehouse and even at one in the afternoon, they still have lunch brisket left. *The perfect illusion of a great day.*

Every bone in my body holds the tension of the day and Collin's hands offer a respite from the cesspool that swirls in my mind. Looking to offload the pain in my back and shoulders, I meld his hands to my pain points, including the one in my heart.

I wonder whether he can feel the blood nervously pumping throughout my body. Every part of me is a drum, beating out a discorded rhythm. *Tell him. Shine the light on the problem to melt it.* I knew when I rather haphazardly joined the Cheater's Club that it really wasn't for me, or for Fielding, and I still don't believe it is. Yet…there's an attraction in saying and doing what you need to do for your own survival without fallout, even if it's an honesty that hounds you a little in the middle of the night with the *probably should haves.*

"Collin, I've been all over the place lately, and I did something I wish I hadn't."

His hands stop in mid-massage. He is very still and his breathing tucks into the space between his throat and lungs, rolling in soft rapid waves. The silence brandishes an unexpected syrupy thick layer of awkwardness between us. *The truth will set you free? Bullshit. The truth hurts.* Interpretation is the only thing that differentiates truths from lies. I gently flip myself to face him.

"I followed you the other day because I just…I couldn't shake the feeling that you weren't being honest about your relationship with Lena. I had a feeling that maybe you thought…maybe you wished things were different. I saw you with her, having lunch, hugging her. Collin, are you attracted to her?"

He clears his throat and does that thing where he pinches the skin in between his eyes. "You followed me? What the hell, Jenna? Why? Didn't we just have this conversation—"

A slurry of anger rises in me and I lose control, propelling myself to sitting like a bullet from a gun. Enunciating every word, I lecture him, "Don't you fucking dare *not* answer my question! Don't you fucking dare answer my question *with* a question! And you didn't even answer this same question the last time I asked you, so fucking answer me!" I scream, my voice pealing through the bedroom.

Collin clamps my shoulders in between his hands and squeezes them until I yelp. "You have to calm the hell down! I haven't done anything with her and I'm not going to, understand?" His pupils dilate as he spits the words through his clenched teeth. "You have to believe me!"

"You didn't answer my question," I reply with no spark in my voice. "Are you attracted to her?"

His eyes mist over and he lets the words precariously tumble through his lips. "Yes. Yes. Yes, I think she's attractive, but there is nothing between us. Jenna, I swear! I promise! I have lunch with her sometimes because we hit it off at the beginning. I consider her a friend—nothing else."

"But in a different time and place?" I query.

"Why do you want to kn—"

"Answer me."

His long arms and legs bound out across the bed in all directions. "You know what, Jenna…you know what? Sometimes I consider what it'd be like to start fresh with someone my own age—nobody else's kids, no age gap understanding to try and close, another person's career who doesn't really understand mine. Yeah, Jenna! I thought about it for a hot second! So what? All this *bullshit* you've been going on about…what about you? What have *you* thought about? An abortion? Graduating from your little fuck boy to someone who's…more like you?" His voice reverberates in his chest and singes my eardrums so that I instinctively cover my ears—and my stomach. "You know what? I don't even care if you've thought that, and you know why? Because I fucking love you! Through it all—all the doubts, everything that's working against us being happy, all the 'what ifs'—it's *all*, every bit of it—because I love you! Besides, do you even really want to know everything…even if you could? I think all any of us could handle is enough of the truth so that we can put our heads on our pillows at night and sleep."

Collin threads his arms around me, stitching me up in his angry love words. I keep my arms nested over my body. "Why did you hug her—more than once?" My breathing is hijacked with my heart hung up in my throat.

"Her mom is sick and she finally had to break down and call hospice. Being a doctor was part of her mother's dream, a dream that she won't really get to see through now. We spend all day laser-focused on solving these complex problems for other people. Sometimes we forget about ourselves. That's all it was."

"Is that all?" I whisper.

"Isn't that enough? Isn't that the kind of kindness you want in a partner? Isn't it enough that I'd give up my whole life for you? I'd die for you, Jenna!"

"I don't want to feel like a sacrifice to you, or a consolation prize. I don't want you to feel trapped, like you have to do your *duty*," I add, the words laced with sarcasm.

"Jenna, I'll gladly do all of those things—and I have to because my whole world revolves around you, our baby, and our family—all of it is *ours*. Fantasies, wondering about how things could be different…isn't that just part of decision making? Isn't that part of being a grown-ass person? I mean, hell…the stakes are high, and I've been adulting hard since I was about twelve. You think I'm completely dense about what this must be like for you?" Collin squeezes me again and punctuates his words with a fierceness that subdues my anger. "Woman, I'm not only here for you; I'm part of you. I'll be your shadow; you'll never know pain, worry, or weariness without me right there beside you. I know we'll have bad times, but I also know we'll have more good than bad. I simply can't imagine going through this shit show we call life without *you* by my side, and I hope you can't imagine it without *me* by *your* side."

I don't answer. I don't have to. I don't have to know his every truth and he doesn't need to know every one of mine. Simply knowing that he accepts me for who I am, who I am not, and who I might want to be is enough. As he holds me, I understand that he's *happy* to be with another human who is imperfect, and one who doesn't hold a permanent role in the shit show. I'm just passing through.

As I drift off into heavy dream, I miss the late night call from his radiologist friend...the call that births a jagged, distraught gurgle from Collin's throat. The call that kept him a prisoner from sleep. The call that ripped his tender heart right from his chest, chased his optimistic dreams from his mind, and tackled his well laid plans to the ground, the four words whirling and dive bombing like an assassin somersaulting to victorious vengeance: *I think it's cancer.*

And he let me sleep...the sleep of the oblivious, the frivolously innocent matted with unappreciated protection.

This is the man I will spend the rest of my life with. I'm done with hunting happy.

****

My week begins on an upward trajectory, except for the Cheater's Club meeting on Friday night—it's my turn to share. I'm debating the devious nature of Elizabeth and how to help Amanda break her. Encouraging temptation...don't know that I'd do it, but I understand the idea of misery wanting company. It's just that when you see it in action, when you see the fallout—someone has to be the solid rock facing that stops that shit in its path. That's me. That's Fielding. That's Shelby Lee. And, maybe that's even Amanda. We will be Elizabeth's swan crash boom song.

On Monday and Tuesday mornings, Collin leaves me notes about what he loves about me—looks, feisty personality, intelligence, kindness. By the time the Wednesday morning sun peeks out from the clouds, I go downstairs to find my favorite pastry and coffee—and him in a t-shirt instead of his shirt and tie.

"Yummy! Finally, a good excuse to eat a crème horn. It's good for the baby, right?" I don't wait for an answer, or investigate why he's not dressed for work, but shove it in my mouth, the crispy layers collapsing around the slightly sweet heavy mascarpone cream filling. After an anticipated swallow, I notice he's looking at me with an odd little smile, enjoying my company while I do nothing except eat. "Are you having one? Why aren't you dressed for work?"

His only answer is a small card—an appointment card he pushes across the kitchen island. It's a breast oncologist and it's for this morning at eleven. "I didn't know how to tell you. You've been so happy, Jenna." His stare is blank, uniformly grieved. "I've been trained how to deliver bad health news. I know I should have told you before, but…in some weird way I thought if I don't say it, maybe it won't come true." He drops the weight of his arms around me and cries. It's the frustrated cry of a life that's been stifled by…life. No one promises those forever blue skies. I know that better than he does simply because I've been orbiting for more time. Older and wiser go together; problems go with a life that's longer in the tooth. Collin slumps to the floor, cupping my belly.

"Will you help me tell the kids?" I ask.

His only response is silence with a ragged sniffle every few seconds, then "Oh God, I didn't think…" trailing behind it. The spring air is summer heavy and there's a dew between my breasts that only stays a few moments with the downdraft from the fan. I once heard someone say that the shortest distance between two people is a laugh. If that's true, tears are too close to measure. Some of the most treasured, tender moments between people are also some of the most tragic. And yet, love prevails…it binds people together with scars and tears and terrible words that sometimes need to be spoken, and then some that should never have to be uttered. I want him to want me…that's on a time limit now. I want him to gaze at me with so much love and desire that he can't see any future unless I'm in it…maybe a future without me will be his only choice. I want him to touch me without fear, without disgust, without regret…without these errant coded cells running amok inside of me. *Why…why when things are so very good, why do I find a flaw? Maybe that's what happens when you're not appreciative…the universe takes it away. Good things are for good people who don't complain, people who can always find a silver lining in their playbook. That's bullshit thinking, right? Then why can't I convince myself of that?*

"I want you to touch me, Collin. Touch me, take me, forget everything in this moment," I beg, brushing his hair away from his face. As the last consonant sounds tumble out of my mouth, the heat from the blood that's filling my nipples descends to a fullness that pulsates deep inside of me. I settle myself into a kitchen chair. Strewn across my lap, he's helpless.

I pull his jaws toward me and rope my tongue around his, penetrating his mouth again and again. My soft lips fall on his, wet with his tears, and pushing into him, our kisses spark that intensity from our first kiss, which seems like a lifetime ago.

Reaching for his hand, I take his finger and collapse my mouth around it; it's slippery wet, a string of spit glowing from the sunlight peeking its way through the blinds. I command his fingers to my every want: tracing my hard nipples and then the wet folds between my legs, slightly entering, but staying their plotted course. And back to my mouth, my jawline, both fingers, diving deep into my throat with a moan that can only come from that place of desire that cannot be extinguished. I press my legs together to stave off the want; the wet anticipation, so strong, slides down my thighs, nearly gluing them together.

His fingers creep back down and detour at my belly. He runs his hands over the smooth protrusion. I know what he's thinking; I'm thinking it, too. And the truth is that I don't care at this moment. I've been liberated by my desire...for *this* man. I'm not thinking of anything else, not engulfed in some fantasy. I'm here. We're living for the now. He runs his lips up the back of my neck, kissing it, biting, until beads of sweat pop out with the goosebumps.

"You belong inside of me," I whisper, pushing his hands between my legs and scissor-squeezing them. I push him back and claim his hand into mine, gently guiding him to the couch in the living room and climb on top of him, making a mess of his hard shaft as I writhe and grind into him while he pulls my hair back, watching me. I'm on a mission—with or without his permission. Gently gliding him inside of me, my pussy collapses upon his whole girth, his entire length and the bliss of that first-in feeling has me clamping down in satisfaction, a trickle of pleasure painting his cock the perfect shade of pride in his ownership of my cunt. My tits are hovering over his open mouth and I pop one in, tantalizing him with the taste of flesh, then the other, his tongue making love to them in sequence to his hips that are bucking under me in the throes of denial. I answer his rhythm by taking the skin of his chin between my teeth, bearing down, nearly ripping it from the bone.

Holding himself up with his muscled abs, Collin draws his hands snug around my rib cage, right under my tits, and uses my hole like an addict—a man with no control. He punch-drunk plunges into me again and again...automatic. There's no talking, no outward tenderness, my body carelessly his...except his eyes. His eyes tell the story of us—friends and fiends, problematic passion, and good match but bad habits...in a sweaty twisted knot of desire that explodes with an atom-bomb intensity that, if I didn't know better, I'd have sworn put his seed in me for a second time.

The tidal wave recedes and we take stock of the toll we've taken in each other's arms, unconsciously willing destruction to the germination of what's probably inside of me. Collin's sweet kiss on my shoulder reminds me of the purgatory that's needing a parachute before it comes crashing in on us.

"When do you want to tell the kids?" he asks.

"As soon as we know something definitive. Will we find out today? Or will there be more tests?"

"This guy will have a good idea. He's one of the best. There will be at least one test...for stage and type. We can tell them as soon as we have that information."

For the first time since my divorce, I cling to Collin, feeling vulnerable.

And mad as hell about it.

Chapter Eleven: A Grain of Sand in Your Crotch

I don't tell anyone about my upcoming appointment with the oncologist. Not my bestie Fielding. Not my children. Not my mother or my father. Collin and I alone nest on this information.

Diagnosis is minutiae. Collin agrees, but contends it's more about making precise steps that inform treatment. I can see that, but it feels like I'm in a hell bound vacuum of doubt over and over again. While I'm glad to have Collin's expertise, I'm also somewhat aggravated by his constant research and probing questions about my lifestyle, family history, and considerations of a variety of treatments. I let it get the best of me and snap during our long wait for the results of the biopsy. "Why do you have your nose stuck in those books when I might die? You should be talking to me…while you still can."

Never looking up, he responds, "I'm not letting you die."

"Maybe you don't have a choice in the matter," I push back.

"But *you* do. Do you want to live, Jenna? If you want to live, you've just won at least half the battle."

"Dr. Craig, c'mon back. Dr. Gregg is ready for you," a nurse announces, her voice floating on my palpable dread.

Dr. Gregg shakes Collin's hand, simultaneously

supporting his arm with his free hand. *A politician's handshake.* He is probably about my age, having practiced long enough to be completely competent, but not so long that he's jaded.

He only addresses me with a friendly cursory glance; his comments roll off his tongue quickly, a burgoo of medical mishmash that Collin filters for me.

"The tumor is stage 3C, invasive ductal carcinoma, grade two. The tumor is four centimeters with likely lymph nodes compromised. For the pregnant patients I've treated, I like to wait until further into the second trimester, and third if we can."

"I want that. I want to wait until I'm about thirty weeks. Can I wait ten weeks to begin treatment?"

Collin whips his head around to me and snarls, "That's over two months! You have a little cancer delivery system being set up in your body right now! No! You can't wait! We can have another baby, we can adopt, we have your kids. *Your* life is more important."

A heat rises inside of me and I yell, "When the hell did you get to make the decision without *me*?"

"Since I'm the only one with a medical degree, Jenna! I know things you don't know."

Dr. Gregg side steps taking a side and offers this: "We can split it down the middle—around twenty-six or twenty-eight weeks. The surfactant in the lungs will be made, which is better if you're having a boy, but better regardless of the sex of the baby. Do we know? Boy or girl?"

Collin grabs my hand, hard, answering him, "We don't know. We wanted to be surprised. I guess we got our surprise, huh?"

I don't look at him when I answer. "I want to be

surprised. I'll find out when the baby is born."

Dr. Gregg closes my file folder and rolls his little stool right in front of me. In what I'm sure is a completely unorthodox move, he lifts my hands into his. "This is not the end of your life, and it's not even the end of your story, unless you want it to be. Finding the right treatment is important, but finding the right attitude is essential."

He turns to Collin and adds, "Remember, do no harm…of any kind. Support should be just that, not pressure. The mother of your child is in an enviable position, having her own in-house doctor, so don't screw it up by trying to play God. I'll bet they never taught you that in medical school, huh? You're welcome," Dr. Gregg sarcastically adds.

Turning his back to Collin, he rotates to face me. "Take care and I'll prep your pre-surgery and lab order. The nurse will be right in. Take care, Jenna." The weight of his feather-light touch brings tears to my eyes—and Collin's, but for far different reasons.

We spend the rest of the time waiting in silence. I'm worried, sad, scared, resentful—and other emotions that I'm not even aware of, those I can't even name. If it weren't for the seething anger that's building inside of me about…*everything*, I think I'd be listless pounds of flesh in the chair.

I have no control.

That's what pisses me off. I'm a pawn, a child's toy restlessly scuttled from place to place. And what is there to do except take your medicine that the universe has you lined up to gulp like a good little girl? If I don't beat this…then what? If I do beat it, then what? I can either see my life as a gilded lily, insurmountably sweetened by the triteness of a come-too-soon death, or I'll be the consummate warrior with a forever pink war stripe zigzagging across my body, chanting for free mammograms and mastectomies.

Either way, I'm pissed. I should be eager to fight. I should be gentle with myself. But, what I am is pissed at the world because I want to feel like the pearl, not the grain of sand. But if I have to feel like the grain of sand, then I guess there's no better place to be than the grain of sand irritating Elizabeth's crotch.

****

Anyone who thinks children are stupid is the king of idiots. Almost as soon as the kids get home from school that day, they know something is rotten. It's hard to paint a perfect picture when your palette is full of grays and blacks. I didn't really plan what to say, other than the truth, which is the only recourse with kids because otherwise, you're left with a liar's identity, which I seem to be pretty good at cultivating lately. *A liar...with cancer...* The words clumsily dive out of my mouth, like cold lumpy oatmeal. I don't even remember saying the words—a disturbing moment in time without a memory attached to it. *Thank God for little miracles.*

Jacob is the only one who cries. "Are you going to die, Mommy?" he stutters. "People with cancer die, don't they? Who will be our Mommy if you die?" He sheepishly snakes his neck around, his eyes landing on Collin.

Collin jumps in to answer. "I'm not gonna let Mom die, buddy." He hooks Jacob around the waist and pulls his little body toward him. I bury my nose in Jacob's hair, and Collin and I hug him until his little body is no longer wracked by sobs.

Vi, unusually quiet, suddenly lashes out at Jacob. "There's medicine they'll give Mom, Jacob! They'll give her medicine that'll make her sick, make her hair fall out, she'll be like a zombie until she's better! And if that doesn't work, they'll chop off her boobs!"

"Vi!" I yell, irritated at her crassness. "Why would you say that? You're scaring him—and me."

"Well, *I'm* scared!" she rallies back, her voice wobbling with anxiety. "I don't want my mom to die! To get cheated out of a good life...we were going to do things together, remember? Girls' trips, matching tattoos...you were going to take me to my first concert, right? Even if you didn't have cancer, now you have a *baby. You* should be scared! What were you thinking, having another kid at your age?"

A kick to the gut...understatement of the year. Out of the mouths of babes. Vi never ceases to surprise me with her wisdom, the truth that I try to hide from her, which she can forage like the rarest truffle. Maybe she has a point...maybe I should cut my losses, have an abortion, let Collin go, and live for myself and my kids. She's not exactly wrong, she just has no reference for what makes all this *right*.

"Vi! We can still do all those things! I will *never* run out of love for you—any of you."

"When will you have *time* for us between a new baby and fighting cancer, Mom? I mean, *really?*"

"I'll always have time for you." Those are the only words I can think of to say. She stomps off up to her room and Collin's light touch on my arm wisely suggests that I stay put to give her some space to process.

Bennett is stoic. He's a thinker. He and Cliff, Fielding's other half, gravitated toward each other when

Bennett was just a little boy—over toy cars. Bennett didn't like playing with them as much as he liked organizing them in his own special way. It was a way Cliff didn't understand, but appreciated and encouraged. Bennett has that same laser focus on a dirty spot on the wall while his lip quivers.

"How serious is it?" he asks, his eyes probing me.

"It's pretty serious. I can't sit back and do nothing. I have to seek treatment very soon."

"What can I do to help?"

It's a simple question without a simple answer, and yet I find one that makes my heart sing. "Bennett, just stay the way you are because you make me so proud," I whisper through tears that will not stop, not that I'd even try.

With his hand outstretched, Bennett, who normally dodges Collin's more overt peacemaking offers, slips into Collin's embrace and lets himself just be…a boy. The boy Collin didn't have the luxury of being. The boy who was scared and angry and who had to grow up too fast because of an adult's selfish decisions…who had to learn to be hard and tougher than the tough times. The boy without a soft place to land who now offers *my* son the respite of grief as a young man caught between wanting to be grown beyond his years and needing to be my son.

Collin holds Bennett, swaying back and forth with him, comforting him. "It's okay, man, it's okay. We're going to fight this with your mom. We're gonna kick cancer's ass and we're gonna be the men who hold her up—you and me. I gotta have you on board man. Will you help me?" Bennett doesn't let him loose, but nods emphatically.

Jacob noodles in between them and pats Bennett's back. My heart is full, even without Vi; she'll come around. But…there's an outlier, a straight-edged honesty that I can't shake, slicing into my heart and mind. *What if I don't make it? What will they do without me? Can they do life without me?*

What makes a path perilous is the lack of a trail. You never know you're going the right way until you get to your destination, which I'm not sure of yet, but maybe my life with the Cheater's Club has to do with cheating death. Either way, this path I'm on will involve the equivalent of slogging around with a grain of sand in *my* crotch, too.

Chapter Twelve: All Truths…Death to Lies

It's easier to keep a secret than to tell the truth. Fielding and I have always had this unspoken code about keeping secrets from each other: Just *don't* fucking do it. It'd be easy to break down. It'd be easy to slump into a fine mess and let her common sense and concern bathe me in relief. It *should* be easy except for this one fact: I'm afraid I'll have to be the strong one.

When she pulls up in the driveway honking, I consider getting annoyed, but *how many more times will I hear that?* Jumping out of the car, she runs to the passenger's side and makes a big deal out of moving the seat back for me. My baby bump has popped. I ply a goofy grin to my face, but that secret wants out.

"Get in, *beeoch*! Look at that cute pooch!" She baby-talks to my stomach and rubs it like she's summoning a genie from a bottle. "Wonder who's sharing this week? I haven't heard anything else out of Shelby Lee."

I stop and put my hands on her shoulders, squarely facing her. "I'm sharing this week."

"Huh?" She grabs me by the elbow before I can fold myself into the seat. "What's going on? You're ch—" She stops short of saying the full word.

"No! I'm not cheating, but I'm going to totally fuck Elizabeth's little world. Don't ask questions. All I need to know is this: You in?"

"Like I said, get in beeoch." She grins and smashes her foot to the floor so hard my *baby* almost gets whiplash.

****

Sometimes, the truth feels like a lie.

I decide solo scorched earth policy is the only way to go with Elizabeth. Fielding has always been on board for any ass-kicking adventure I could concoct, but this…this needs to be me because I don't take it lightly, people fucking with my family. I may not be able to kick cancer's ass, but I sure as shit can take care of the head bitch of the Cheater's Club. *Burn bitch, burn.*

Fielding guns the engine and hops the curb, demolishing a bank of exquisitely trimmed boxwoods. "Ooops," she groans, turning to me with a huge grin on her face and even bigger sunglasses. "Who do I look like, Thelma or Louise?"

"You look like you, except the total badass version. You know what?"

"You brought brass knuckles?"

"Damn! I knew there was something I was forgetting." I wrap my hand over hers. "I am *really* proud of you for not giving in and cheating. I'm certainly no angel, and I'm not a judgmental prude either, but I don't think that's you. I don't think that would have made you truly happy, or satisfied."

"Yeah, you know what I realized? I don't need to screw someone else for Cliff to love me. And, I don't need to screw anybody else for me to love *myself* either. Love is good, but there are so many kinds of love, and I think the best kind is loving yourself. It's good to see yourself through a different lens, without any love except your own. I think maybe that's what Elizabeth's missing.

We probably should pity her."

A long silence languishes between us, and we both simultaneously conclude, "Hell no." We don't knock, but parade on in and immediately make eye contact with a wild-eyed Amanda who is being chastised by Elizabeth for some minor faux pas.

"Well, my favorite duo! Ladies, you're fashionably early," she mews, arranging an enormous bouquet of lilies. "I can't imagine why I'd be so lucky." Her words drip with sarcasm and I can imagine that she's guardedly aware of our unusual intimacy.

"I'm sharing today, Elizabeth," I warn.

She drops a lily, and her gaze, toward me. "You are. *You* are? Well, isn't this a stroke of pleasure I never expected from you." She returns to her work, mumbling to herself.

We make small talk until Landy, the new woman Sarai, Shelby Lee's replacement, and Shelby Lee bop in, innocently unaware of the trajectory the Cheater's Club will take today. My heart beats fast and my hands are wet with anticipation; I marvel at what's growing inside of me—not the baby or the cancer, but the feeling that maybe…I'm way past due—shrug off the beta and command my alpha side. Fielding catches my eyes and overemphasizes her breathing, patting my knee, as if to say, *Let's do this.*

Shelby Lee rushes in alongside us, her face flushed, and takes her seat. Leaning over she warns, "Michelle will be here soon. You got fifteen minutes tops before hell breaks loose."

Elizabeth sashays to the center of our circle and unwittingly announces her undoing. "Ladies, welcome to the Cheater's Club…where secrets are safe and lies become liberation.

"I want to welcome our newest member, Sarai, whom I've had the pleasure of recruiting. One in, one out is our mantra, and Shelby Lee is moving on with her little happy ending, shall we say?" Elizabeth's mouth holds a dour shape as her veiled ridicule continues to flow across the room. "When Fielding first showed up, I understood that her motives were not so unlike any of ours—finding freedom in fantasy. One of the finest traits humans have the ability to use imagination, creativity. It just happens that we use it for our own pleasure.

"And Jenna? I bristled at her arrival—Fielding's quasi-conjoined twin." She cackles and raises her eyebrows my way. "But what I've come to appreciate about Jenna is her aptitude for change. When she first stepped foot in this sanctuary, she was an optimistically jaded woman, trying to have the foolishly contrived fairy tale life.

"However, with my help, she's, quite literally, seen the truth about love," Elizabeth tilts her head next to mine...*as if she knows anything about the truth,* "and I think she's metamorphosed into something I can live with, something more akin to being a worthy addition to the Cheater's Club. Don't you think, dear?" Elizabeth clutches both my hands, helping me to my feet, and escorts me to the center—with her.

She raises her glass, "To Jenna!"

Everyone raises a glass, even Amanda, who raises a glass to me secured behind the massive arrangement of gladiolus. Holding her breath and her glass in the air a little too long, Fielding awkwardly stands between me and the small gathering. She silently mouths "You don't have to do this" which I ignore because I definitely have to do this—for me and for her.

I put my hand on my belly to steady myself and breathe deeply.

"I have to admit that when I attended my first meeting, I didn't really understand the truths that could be gleaned from all the lies. Perhaps I didn't appropriately appreciate the beauty, the freedom in the deceit. Whatever it was, I have seen the light, as they say," I twirl the stem of my glass between my fingers and add, "and I've heard some even hotter stories. Bravo ladies!" I raise my own glass and everyone follows.

"There's nothing like some good ole fashioned fucking, is there?" Elizabeth cuts her eyes around to me. While no one would ever accuse her of being a prude, she's not supportive of crass speech for the sake of, so I make my words and ideas as common as possible. "And a lot of what happens in our little club is fucking *with* people's minds, but that's not what you need to do. Yeah, everybody understands you gotta fuck him in totally random places, give him road head, send not-safe-for-work pictures, tell him what a wet slutty mess you are just thinking about him. But ladies, don't fuck *with* his mind. Fuck him *in* his mind first! You'll have him eating his own cum out of your hands."

Fielding snorts and guffaws, covering her mouth with her hand at my wise words, and at Elizabeths' glare.

"Dear, perhaps concentrate more on the details and less on the philosophy behind them. A first name might be nice."

"A name? You want a name? I'll give you a name. I'll give you multiple names."

Sarai gasps and Landy hoots, clapping, as I continue. "Lover. Friend. Partner in crime. Hot dick ride.

My ride or die, my husband-to-be, my soul mate, and father of my future child."

Elizabeth jumps up from her perch and hisses, "This isn't what we do here! We do not talk about love! No one wants to hear about your perfect life!" She continues spitting words at me. "Love is not allowed, Jenna. Lust— lust. Happy endings are figments of your imagination, wisps of a too-forgone fairy tale."

"Maybe for you Elizabeth, but not for everyone. You think you've chosen the easy way out, but what you've really chosen is pain and suffering—mostly for yourself, except for this little club where you offload all that shit on to other people. Love is no fairy tale; that idea is for pathetic, weak sops. Love is tears and sacrifice and sometimes it's dishonesty, and sometimes it's even worse than that. But for two people who want it and are willing to work through all the bullshit to get to the golden hour, it's a road worth walking. And it will *always* be worth it."

"It will *never* be worth it!" Her words are succinct, punctuated with an exacting revenge. The red lipstick bleeds outside the cupid's bow of her lips.

"It's a shame that rage and hurt have blinded you to the fact that you can be happy without destroying yourself and other people. You think you're stuck in a loveless marriage? Hell, you don't even love yourself enough to listen to anything I'm telling you. Isn't that the definition of insanity?" I look to my audience for support.

Elizabeth hurls her highball glass toward my body and Fielding pushes me out of the way. I slide to the floor onto my butt, landing in between Fielding's legs.

"You fucking bitch! You hurt my friend, and you'll

never have to worry about your fucking pathetic life again because I'll end it for you," Fielding delivers her threat with tight lips and fists, a somber, calm lilt in her voice. She pounces on Elizabeth, and collars her wrist, but the weight of the eyes on her gives her enough composure to release it.

The doorbell blings hard two times, an insistent ringer at the door. We hear Michelle's shrill voice mixed with anger and tears, accusing Elizabeth of treachery.

"*You* claimed to offer a safe spot for our indulgences…that's what you said! You're a liar! If I'm ruined, then so are you!"

Elizabeth's voice never rises to anything but a loud whisper and an adrenaline-exhausted Landy peeks into the kitchen, hardly acknowledging us. Sparks of anger are palpable in the air and Michelle sweeps her hand across the hall table, knocking the vase of flowers across the floor. The stunning sound of glass cracking and spinning across the floor sweeps a chill up my spine.

A well formed vein pops out on the side of her neck as she explains herself to Elizabeth at a decibel well above what Elizabeth is likely used to when people speak to her. "Someone *recorded* the last time I shared and sent the file to John! He called off our engagement…he dumped me—*me*! *This* is why I'm upset! *You*," she puts her finger on Elizabeth's chest, "are supposed to prevent that from happening. In fact, how the *fuck* does that even happen? How, Elizabeth?"

Michelle turns around to us and quizzes us. "Who did this? I know there's a rat here and I'll find that bitch out! *Who* did this?" She is ravenous, a fiend: red in the face and frazzled, her dark eyes dilated and wild with the desire to destroy someone.

"Now, Michelle, you know I'd *never* do anything to compromise a club of my own making, which gives me air in these very lungs." She points to herself. "But, you missed quite the show by someone who *would* do that. Jenna Craig gave a remarkable soliloquy—she's got the motive and the spirit behind the action."

Elizabeth points her finger my way. "This bitch has come to play so I say we show her our balls."

"Flag on the play, ladies."

An unfamiliar, yet determined voice floats over the air, cutting a swath through Michelle's rage, landing squarely at Elizabeth's feet.

"What did you just say to me?" Elizabeth seethes over the vase of flowers at Amanda.

"I said, 'Flag on the play, ladies,' which means—"

"I know what it means!" Elizabeth bellows, her fury ringing through the foyer. "How *dare* you even deign to speak to me—"

"Go to hell, Elizabeth. Do you mean you don't like it when I speak to you like that? And that recording? All me—and I've got more, too. So, unless you potentially want to be unemployed, back the hell off, Michelle. And remember, you can be a whore without being an unkind human."

Michelle pushes through us, huffing, and heads out the door. Landy collects her purse from the console table and turns to Elizabeth. "I'm going home. There's nothing here for me anymore. I will have no job at the end of the semester, and—*possibly* no prospects of one in academia again. Soon I'll be without a husband, which I guess is for the best. It's a relief I don't have to be the one to end it. And you can no longer offer what I wanted most: acceptance of and security in who I think I truly am. I guess the next logical step is to leave the Cheater's Club. Goodbye, Elizabeth."

Elizabeth says nothing at all. She pushes the white skunk chunk of hair off of her face and makes several attempts at deep breathing. She watches Landy leave, then turns back to Amanda. "I gave you a soft place to land when no one else would. I loved you when everyone else utterly detested you. I—"

"*You* took advantage of me when I was at my lowest. *You* manipulated me until I couldn't even see any version of myself that I recognized. You offered me a job as your *maid* when you could have offered me anything, or *everything* else. You…" Amanda trailed off.

Elizabeth interrupts, "*You took* everything else! *You* made my husband fall in love with you! And to add insult to injury, he told me he *wanted* you *instead* of *me!*" Elizabeth's truth eked out along with tears that looked very much out of place on her hard, lined face.

Amanda cautiously steps out from behind the kitchen island. "We were friends once, you and I. Remember?"

Elizabeth's icy, teary-eyed stare not only gives no recollection, but no desire to reconnect with that memory. Her angry deep breaths punctuate her refusal.

"It was our own little Cheater's Club, gone terribly wrong, wasn't it?"

"It didn't have to. You and *my* husband allowed yourselves to indulge your feelings. What a completely shitty thing to do." Elizabeth enunciates every syllable of her accusation. "You never apologized. I never would have guessed you to be such a rude little bitch."

"I never guessed that you would have been so hurt. It was your idea—swapping spouses. You never even acted like you cared much for Roger, taking every opportunity you had to bash him to me."

"Oh! And I can only imagine how that made for some delicious pillow talk between the two of you! It serves you right, losing everything, including everything and everyone you loved. And for what? Unrequited love?"

"Roger did love me, Elizabeth!"

"Not enough to lose half his fortune, Amanda! And so, you…guilt-ridden and conscientious…let Anthony have it all. Your millionaire's wife life—gone. You thought you'd just move in on mine, did you? Anthony possessed more hutzpah than I gave him credit for having. What a pity you have none." She chuckles. "In fact, I suppose you'd have nothing, if it weren't for me, paying you a ridiculous salary for a *maid*."

"Why did you offer me a job in your home?" Amanda queries.

Elizabeth traces the rim of her glass with her finger and asks, "Why did you take it?"

Amanda drops her chin to her chest and sighs. "I needed a job, of course, and…part of me thought that if I served you, it would somehow make things right. I don't know why I didn't apologize. But, maybe it's not too late."

Elizabeth smacks her hands together and belly laughs. "My sweet, little fool! You think a seven-year apology would even scratch the surface of my wound? On the surface it would seem that I had some pity for you. I decided that if I had to suffer, then you and Roger would as well.

"My husband was not in love with me any longer, but didn't have the nerve, or the dignity, to do anything about it. Can you even calculate the torture of living with that truth every day? I surmised that I would make sure that he was tortured every day of his life, and you, too. Keep your friends close and your enemies closer…how did I do? I hadn't anticipated that he would take every international flight he could get, or every flight attendant who would spread her legs…every opportunity to stay away from me—and you. Voila…the Cheater's Club Redux."

"I'm sorry, Elizabeth. I'm sorry I have a heart and that you don't," Amanda whispers through tears.

Elizabeth goes to Amanda and envelops her in what looks like a hug, but similar to a constrictor snake, I'm not sure whether she's embracing her or emboldened by Amanda's felicitous remorse. "I didn't count on your treachery a second time. Shame on me."

Weaving the words that transmit a shockwave of truth: the Cheater's Club is Elizabeth's swan song of revenge. It never had anything to do with anyone else's pleasure. It was a crucible by which she transformed her pain.

Everyone freezes as if in a child's game of tag. Sarai, along with Shelby Lee, had made their getaway, letting the door slam behind them, long before now, likely never to return. Fielding and I begin to fidget. *Do we run or stay and stomp out what's left of the Cheater's Club?* A sudden urge to pee busts my resolve to stay. I grab at Fielding's sleeve. "Let's go. I think Amanda's got it— she's the one who needs to finish this."

Before we get in the car, I squat in the bushes while Fielding plucks a small bunch of blooms from a huge hydrangea in the yard. "I don't know what got into you," she calls toward me, "but damn, girl! I liked it!" She pumps her bicep up and down toward me as I emerge.

I stop to smell the flowers and reveal, "Cancer. That's what's gotten into me. Fucking cancer."

****

"What? What do you mean?" Fielding tightly grips the steering wheel, shaking her head in disbelief as she backs out. "No. No, they're not right Jenna. That's some bullshit mistake. They looked at the wrong file, wrong boobs. Total bullshit."

"They have the right file, right boobs."

Her eyes fill and her knuckles fade white. Her head shakes back and forth, refusing my words as part of her reality now. "Nope. No, not true."

"It's true. I'm sorry."

"Where? Is it…" Fielding hunts for the right word, but settles on "bad?"

She never takes her eyes from the road.

"Breast. Remember the lump? It wasn't just a milk duct. The doctor thinks it's probably moved into my lymph system. It's not terrible. I'll likely survive, but it's going to involve a fight. My treatment has to start soon."

She slings the car to the shoulder of the road, flinging off her seat belt. Fielding leans in close to me and puts her face close to mine. "What do you mean *likely*? You *will* fight and you *will* win because I won't have it any other way. Fuck this shit," she whispers, swerving back onto the road. "This is *our* fight now. Fuck. This. Shit. Cancer is a motherfucker—a motherfucker who's going down.

"Fuck this shit," she quietly repeats to herself.

I softly touch her arm, locked in a hard line. "Fielding, I couldn't decide the right time to tell you. It's okay if you're mad or upset. I get it. Sometimes I feel *everything* and sometimes I just feel numb, as if I'm waiting at the deli for someone to call my number and take my order…like 'Gimme the pastrami with a fucking schmear of cancer.'"

Fielding's mouth opens and the loudest cackle I've ever heard erupts from her mouth, which slowly turns into a breathless sigh and inconsolable wailing. We sit on the shoulder of the road from eye-searing early evening sun through dusk.

"You know," I say, "I'll bet between the two of us we could legitimately fill a gallon jug with the tears we've cried over all the things. You just added about a quart."

"I want to do something…before your treatment."

"Okay! I need to get my phone and look at the calendar—"

"No, I mean now! Let's start driving and see where we get to. Tonight. You can sleep and I'll stop to get some rot gut coffee, and we'll just drive."

"Just like Spring Break '98? We stopped and washed our panties in the sink at every scuzzy gas station between here and Florida because we forgot to pack any clean ones!"

"I didn't forget," she chimes in, beaming from ear to ear.

"I didn't either. I love you, Fielding."

"I know. If you die, I can't love you anymore. So, you can't die."

"I'm gonna try not to, *beeoch,*" I laugh, "Sometimes I'm stubborn, I guess…I forget I have a lot to live for. So, where are we going?"

Fielding sits up in the driver's seat and rubs her hands together. "Really?! You're up for it? I thought you'd be a party pooper and make me take you home."

"What I have at home can wait twenty-four hours. No one's gonna die without me. Ugh...no pun intended."

"I want to stop at a truck stop diner and eat pie."

"I like, no, I *love* pie. Pie is perfect! Then what?"

"I want to stand on the side of a mountain and look at the stars and the moon. I want to feel *infinitesimal*— hand it all over to someone else to control. Maybe we can pray?"

"Uhm...okay! I've read that prayer is proven to be beneficial. It's been a hot second since I've *really* prayed, so this is probably a great time to start. I actually like that idea...someone else in control. That's not nearly twenty-four hours, though. What else?"

"Let's skinny dip in the ocean!"

"There's not an ocean close enough! How about Lake Rebo?"

"Nah, everybody's done that. I know! Let's go find a bar—and just dance like fools, then we stay at a no-tell motel, talk and laugh and sleep right beside each other, and get up early enough to see the sun rise with the best damn cup of coffee we can find."

"Can we maybe upgrade to a Hilton? I don't wanna get bed bugs."

"Yaaasss, girl!" Her eyes fill up with tears again. "I just want to make some more memories with you...while we can. I know we should do something glamorous. This isn't much of anything."

"You're wrong, Fielding. It's *everything*."

****

Fielding pulled the steering wheel hard, right into the lot of the Motor Park Cafe where I had pecan pie and homemade vanilla ice cream with the real vanilla bean bits, and Fielding had an obnoxious amount of whipped cream with a side of cherry pie, which made her think about the song of the same name by the band Warrant. We watched the video and bemoaned the fact that we'll never look that comely again and that the lead singer is dead. *Dead...its timing will kill ya.*

About twelve miles down the road we found a place to pray—a lonely spot off the highway where we saw Ursa Minor and a shooting star. Fielding prayed like I had never heard her pray before, half threatening, and promising we'd *both* be kind to the worst, snobbiest people, including Elizabeth, serve as earth-bound angels for the hopeless and destitute, then swore off anything sexual that didn't involve Cliff or Collin *if...*I could be cured.

From the tippy top of our gilded perch we spied a honky tonk at the river's edge, partially carved into the side of the mountain face. We heard it before we saw it. Dwight Yokam's "A Thousand Miles From Nowhere" called to us (we both swore it was a sign) and Fielding put a quick amen on the prayer. She said God already knew what she wanted, what she needed, and she didn't think he'd appreciate any half-hearted words...even from her. But he'd totally appreciate our enjoying music beside the Jehovah's Witnesses ladies who sneaked out to have a good time, including accompanying me, squatting to pee, in the makeshift gravel parking lot.

We laughed, we danced, they drank, and I marveled at the world I'd forgotten existed: the world of contentment. We settled on a tidy little Rome Inn where we cuddled in the lumpy bed and put our ears to our neighbors' wall laughing at a cacophony of snoring and farting.

These are the memories I pack into my soul, wrapping them around me like a familiar blanket into the next months that will surely be the hardest of my life.

Chapter Thirteen: Walk the F*ck Away…Then Come the F*ck Back

It's week twenty—the halfway point of the pregnancy, and the countdown week to surgery.

"Have you thought about names?" Collin asks, sipping on his coffee and rubbing my feet that are lazily propped in his lap.

"No. I've been too busy thinking about putting off chemo and opting for surgery instead. I'm wondering whether I've made the wrong decision." I offer him a disgusted look. "I just want this shit the hell out of me."

"Are you worried about what I think?"

"Yeah, maybe. I want to give this baby a chance. This feels right to me, but I know you disagree."

"Patients go against medical advice all the time, but your *doctor* was willing to work with you. I'm practically your husband and I'll support you no matter what."

The smile on my face cannot match the one that's pasted on my heart, traveling to my jellylike knees and tingly toes. "I have no words for how wonderful you've been. You're an old soul, you know that? In a yummy shell. There's no one else who could handle this, handle me."

"Fielding?"

"She's missing the yummy shell that I like to eat."

"Oooh! You didn't mention you'd be eating my

shell!" Collin laughs and repositions my legs, and I can feel his junk and massage it between my feet. He grins and squeezes my feet to stop me. "I love you. You couldn't do anything to make me stop loving you. Wrong things, right things—doesn't matter. You'll always be that flame I'll never extinguish, even if I could."

"What do you think about Evelyn or Esther?"

He scratches at the scruff on his face, which is turning me on. "Ah, Evelyn is okay but Esther is too traditional. Why'd you just go with girl names?"

"I'm awful with boy names. I feel like it's a girl, though." I cut my eyes around to him. "You know, don't you?"

Smiling, he adds, "Yeah, and you'll never get it out of me."

"Oh really?" I dig my toes into his balls with just the right pressure.

"Woman, don't start something you can't finish."

"Who says I can't finish? You know damn good and well I'm not a quitter."

I dip my big toe into the waistband of his shorts, prompting him to shimmy them off, down to his thighs. Putting the balls of my feet together, I stroke his shaft. His head falls back as he gets harder. I spin around in my seat, checking to see if any of the neighbors are out, not that they could see much, but even if they could, it adds to the excitement.

"I think we need some lube," I say, crawling between his legs and wrapping my mouth around his cock, which I lick like one of those giant lollipops at a candy store—enjoying every ridge, swirling my tongue across the tip until he's dripping with a mix of his sugar and my spit.

"Don't you stop," he warns, giving a nervous look through the tree line.

"Not a chance," I volley back, smacking the side of his ass cheek, to get his attention.

Balancing on the edge of my seat, I find a grip and a rhythm that produces an open-mouthed smile. His cock is silky wet between my feet and I like watching him get worked up, his face contorting into iterations of pleasure and pain. He flexes his legs, tightening the muscles; his breathing is ragged, but determined. "Come for me, Daddy," I whisper.

Writhing in his seat, he quietly moans, clasping his hands around my feet so that the grip is tighter, more intense, and he directs the rhythm.

"Gimme that good cum all over my toes. C'mon baby," I coax.

We lock eyes and I am wet watching him on the verge of coming from desire and fear. With his eyes fluttering between open and closed, he grunts once and a warm sticky glob covers the bottom of my feet; his back is arched and the muscles in his beautiful, strong legs and arms pop with his release.

He comes down with a devilish grin on his face, snatching me to my feet and pulling me toward his lap. "You and your kinky feet! Would you get me a paper towel or a tissue…Delil…uh, I mean Jenna?"

"Huh?" I pull back, my mind wrapped in confusion. "Wait…huh? What name did you start to call me?"

Shock is plastered on his face and my heart drops, only to be ripped back up a hill like a roller coaster. "Delilah. My girl name…*our* girl name."

"The baby's name? That's your girl name pick?"

"Yeah," he plows through the word, catching his

breath.

"What's your boy name?" I ask.

"Don't have one."

I sit back on his lap and pull his head to my heart. *We're having a daughter!* "You aren't disappointed we're not having a son? A boy?"

"No, because I know our daughter will be as beautiful as you. How could I be upset about that? And I have two great sons."

"I like that name. How'd you settle on it?"

"I wanted something that ended like your name, but unique. I stumbled on Delilah and couldn't get it out of my mind. You like it?"

"It's perfect," I whisper in his ear, wondering whether he's being honest or just quick on his feet.

An awkward silence passes between us. "You thought that was another woman's name I accidentally said, thinking about her?" I don't answer, or look at him, so he gently twists my face to his. "Did you think that?"

I nod my head.

"This is going to kill us if you can't shake the feeling that I'm not being faithful. We can't start our marriage like this."

Completely without thinking I blurt out, "I've not been honest with *you* about something."

He slowly sits down, his face blanched, likely wondering what horrific truth I'm about to pile drive him with to destroy his perfect moment. He sits, his arms crossed against his chest, waiting for the pummel to the heart.

"You know Fielding is separated from Cliff and she got this invitation to join a club—The Cheater's Club. It's pretty much the way it sounds…I went with her for support—many times. We didn't cheat, but we listened to stories from women who did. There's this woman named Elizabeth who's the organizer. I think she's…evil—a total bitch."

"How many times did you go?" he asks, his lips stiff with disgust.

"We only went three or four times. The last time we went, Fielding and I imploded the whole thing. That bitch needed to be stopped." My words echo in my ear and with my nervous eyes I hang on to his.

"Wait a minute. So, you lied to me, you went to a cheating club, all the while accusing *me* of doing shit, and you expect me to believe that this was a rescue mission?"

A sudden fluttering in my stomach catches me off guard and I grab Collin's hand, putting it on my stomach. He briefly smiles, and pulls his hand away. And I yank it back.

"I'm not a child. I'm not that easily distracted. That's a beautiful thing, but this…*this* is not. You *lied* to me—multiple times. I was honest with you about Lena when you asked, even though I thought maybe I shouldn't be 'cause I wasn't doing anything wrong."

An angry surge beats in my chest and skips to my brain. "Yeah, I know you didn't *do* anything wrong, but you thought about it—just like me! So, maybe I should have told you, but *I* didn't do anything wrong either. So we're square, right?" *Damn the truth. Damn the truth!*

"I don't know what to say. I think I just need some time, Jenna." He quietly gets up and walks across the deck to the edge.

"Fielding will tell you the same thing!" Reaching for his arm, I attempt to draw him back in. "We're not cheaters! You know that, right? Thinking about it is not the same as doing it."

"I'm not sure what I know anymore. And why would I ask Fielding? She *is* a cheater, remember what you told me? Sorry, Jenna, but I don't have a lot of faith in what *she* would tell me. Hell, I'm not even sure about what you've told me."

"Then walk away, Collin. Just walk away, Mister Perfect! Mister The-rules-don't-apply-to-me! I sure as hell know I'm not perfect—never claimed to be. And I can admit it. There are only a few things I know for sure in this suck-ass world: I love my children, I'm having *your* daughter, I love Fielding, warts and all, and I love you. Love is not perfection. Love is not the penultimate destination; it's a freaking journey, a full swamp of shit to get through. I'm being honest. I'm taking a risk because today is the day *we* move forward—*we're* having a baby, *we're* getting married, *we're* battling cancer. You have responsibilities, and I have hope—in us, in our life together. So, if you're going to walk away, then just fucking do it today. Either fight for this now, or walk the fuck away."

"I'm not the kind of man who just gives up, Jenna! I won't be that man."

"Are you sure? Because your dad sure was!" *Fuck. I said it…the words he probably thought he'd never hear, he never wanted to hear: He's like his father.*

Collin English turns his back and walks away.

****

Collin and Fielding take me to my surgery appointment, although he and I have hardly talked in twenty-four hours. They fuss like an old couple over what I should wear, the drinks and snacks that would taste good and be nutritious, and aftercare—will Collin take care of me or will Fielding take charge? I just sit back and bitterly laugh, rubbing my belly, because these worries are for people whose lives are not imploding.

My parents are camped out at my house with the children. It's one big happy time—except for cancer. It's the visitor no one wants, but everyone has to endure. *I wonder what torture it is to watch your child fight for her life? How is it to watch your parents thrive while you die?* I try to push the thought out of my brain. Worrying over what other people are thinking and feeling is the kiss of death—and I'm precariously close.

Fielding helps me to the car where Collin is waiting—alone—behind the wheel. I stop at the trunk of the car, peddling for something that will keep me out of the front seat beside him. "My back is hurting a little…you think you could ride up front with Collin? Stretching my legs out might help."

"Well, of course! And I'll even keep my hands to myself." She snorts and I strain to laugh.

"You okay?" she asks, rubbing my shoulder. "You know everything is going to go well. You have a great surgeon, you're healthy, the baby is healthy. He'll go in, chop those babies right off, then you can get some ginormous titties, make everyone jealous at the pool next summer." Fielding brushes the hair away from my face. "And you have an aftercare team that fucking rocks," she adds.

Gulping hard, I stare at her through dry, rapid blinks. "I'm really lucky. I know. I'm just nervous, that's all."

She helps me lower into the back seat. "That's understandable."

Collin doesn't acknowledge me, and I don't

acknowledge him. Fielding chatters away about everything—Cliff's new job, their progress at therapy, meals she'll bring over after my parents leave—anything and everything I should be interested in, but I can only concentrate on one shitty feeling: *Maybe I've driven him away for good?*

Collin concentrates on every turn and stops at every light with careful precision. I watch his eyes in the rear view mirror, hoping for a glance that will let me know we're okay—or even better than okay. *But I am a ghost.*

Fielding stops mid-sentence and whips around to look at me and then bends far around to see Collin's face. "What the hell is going on with you two? You've not said anything to me this whole car ride, and in fact, I don't even think you've said anything to each other." She pauses and adds, "What gives? This is bad fucking mojo to go into surgery with."

"There's no such thing as mojo before surgery." Collin's voice is empty.

"Oh, there sure as hell is!" Fielding counters. "And *this,* whatever this is, *this* is bad mojo. I can't, no I *won't* let the surgery happen unless we all talk. You're both being totally *weird.*" The words stick to the roof of her mouth like turned milk. "Get your shit worked out."

"I told him about the Cheater's Club."

"Ohhhh." Fielding shifts the seatbelt across her chest and hums. I watch her lick her lips. "You know, we didn't actually cheat, Collin. In fact, you would have been so proud of—"

Collin interrupts, "Proud? Proud of my wife-to-be for lying about being in a club for women who cheat? You've lost your damn mind, Fielding! Or wait…maybe you were exactly in the right spot, huh?" His knuckles bear down on the wheel, whipping his eyes square on her.

I know Fielding better than I know any human on earth. And this look is the gasoline to her molotov. I have *never, ever* heard her scream as loudly as she screams at Collin.

"Pull the hell over, you little snot-nosed *bitch*!"

His knuckles jump off the wheel at her command, skidding to a stop that nearly puts me on the floorboard.

She snarls, "You...*you* think you have some right to judge what I do? You think you've got it all figured out, huh? Well, fuck you, Collin English! You naïve bastard! I've done some shit and I'll admit it to anyone who will listen, not to brag, but to say, 'Hey...life is a mixed bag, but learn from it and don't let it destroy you.' That doesn't mean I deserve some shitty label from *you*. You got lucky—you were able to walk away before it got too hot. What about next time? And there will be a next time. Did you even bother to fucking ask Jenna *why* she went?"

"No." His eyes blink heavy as he presses his back into his door, building his knees as a barrier to Fielding.

"She went to make sure I didn't do anything stupid!" she screams again. "And you know why? Because she's a *good* fucking person who *cares* about people!" Fielding pushes her finger into his chest. "She did that for *me!* She didn't want to go. She said it was a bad idea from the get-go. She didn't like Elizabeth—pegged her right from the beginning. But she was patient and...she was my *friend.* And now, *you* want to be a judgmental jerk? *You* want to act like the problem is that Jenna lied? No, asshole, that's not the problem. The problem is that you couldn't handle the truth about how good she really is! And maybe that's because you've got a little secret piece of your dad in you, huh? A secret piece of shit?"

She directs her softened ire to me next. "I love you, but stress and hormones aside, you're being a stubborn bitch. Let him in. Not all guys suck. The conversations we have…maybe also have them with this guy," she points to Collin, "If you love him, and if you know he *loves* you, and he *does*," she stretches her neck back around to him, pointing, "then open your heart when you open your mouth. And then… open your legs." She sits up straight in her seat, eyes pasted forward on the road.

My hand hovers over his shoulder, and then Collin's hand meets it in mid-air. "I'm sorry I lied. I want you to believe me—everything, and especially that I want you, and only you."

"Jenna, of course I want our future together to include love, but fueled by honesty and respect. Maybe I haven't told you enough how much I love you because you never stop impressing me. I…maybe, I thought you might not need me as much as I need you. I've been trying to figure out how—*if*—I fit into your life."

"But you do, even if it feels like I shove you away only to yank you back. It's hard to trust. It's harder to trust myself."

His eyes blink heavy with tears. "Damn…those words about my dad—those cut."

"I know. I'm sorry. I felt judged and I was pissed, then I acted like an asshole."

"I don't blame you for being pissed, even though the only place I've been morally gray has been in my mind."

"Me too. And I haven't been easy to live with lately."

"The truth?" He twirls the engagement ring on my

finger. "Sometimes, I wonder if I'll be like my dad and," his voice wobbles, "be the asshole who messes up a pretty damn wonderful life. I don't want to do that."

"Then come the fuck back."

****

My groggy eyelids shutter open and closed. The quiet is eerie and I wonder if this space is the in-between of two worlds, where people either stay or cross over…maybe beg for forgiveness or die in steely denial. My ears pick up a familiar sniffle: Fielding.

I snake my arm out from under the warm hospital blankets and find Fielding's leg, which I squeeze. "Hey…for a hot second I thought I was in heaven, but then I looked over and saw you, *sooo*…where's your pitchfork?"

She leans over and drapes her arms across my pelvis, gently hugging me. "You have to get better. It's not time for you to leave, Jenna!"

I comb through her hair, aware of her worry. "Bitch, I'll wait for you at the Pearly Gates. I heard they give out golden thongs and pasties, plus fuck me sandals with little wings."

"That's not what I mean!" she hisses through tears that burst and roll down her face like fat bubbles blown from a child's toy wand. "Jenna, what if you're sick because of me? What if this is payback, some sort of karmic retribution?"

"Fielding, that's ridiculous! I don't think that's how karma or cancer work. You're intelligent. You know this is just a crappy, sucky thing that happens to people sometimes."

"But you don't have family history, and you eat well and exercise," she rushes through her words and blubbers through tears, "This shouldn't be happening to you!" She twists the blanket in her hand and strikes the bed with her balled up fist. "This should be happening to me. *I'm* the one with the family history. *I'm* the one who still eats breakfast out of the work vending machine, and drinks swill like I should be drinking water. *I'm* the one who wanted to go to the Cheater's Club. It should be me. I deserve this, not you. Not you! Not *you*, Jenna."

"Fielding, stop...you're projecting. You're just feeling guilty, and for what? You haven't even done anything. Well, except the girl-on-girl friskies, which any guy would find hot. That's a turn-on story for somebody out there." A gentle, controlled laugh rolls out of my belly and I put my free hand on my chest. A flat, bandaged mess cocoons my torso. *They're gone.* Then, a hand on my belly. *I forgot—just for a few minutes.* A separate, rapid beep, out of time from my own heart monitor, reminds me of the life inside of me who will experience every blow I do. *Which one of us will survive it, though? Can I be strong enough for both of us?* "Fielding, is the baby...okay?"

"Yes! God...yeah, the baby's fine! And *you're* fine...you're going to be better than fine because I'm getting my shit straight, Jenna. I can't do this anymore. I can't stand seeing this happen to you." She sits up and wipes her face, resolutely claiming, "If I turn over a new leaf, everything will be okay. It'll go away. Everything will be like it was." Her eyes land heavy on my chest and we both startle at the heavy plodding footsteps of the nurse who asks me how I feel and by the look on my face, decides to dose me with more pain meds.

"Look, Ma! No titties!" I smile, holding my hands only slightly in the air. It's impossible to put them up too much from the pain. I rest them on my baby belly.

"I'll help you, you know. I'll cook dinner. I'll do laundry. I'll get up with the baby, give bottles, change diapers, I'll help with the kids—they can stay with me. I'd do anything for you, *anything* for you to get better." Fielding plies me with a longing gaze, as if it's a poker move and I hold control over the cards.

"Just promise me you'll take care of Collin, too?"

"Of course!"

"You can give him hand jobs…maybe a blow job thrown in for good measure."

"Jenna…gawd…well, speak of the damn sexy devil," she curses, roughly dabbing at the tears under her eyes.

I catch a fuzzy outline draping himself over the side of my bed. He swarms me with gentle kisses and caresses, but even through the medicine haze I can tell he's upset. His eyes are red-rimmed and when he pulls his mask down I see that his face is tear-blotched.

He rests his hands on top of mine, swaddling our baby.

"Hey you…" I murmur, fighting to stay lucid. "What's that?" I take my tipsy fingertip and trace his fading face from my bed. His silence makes my heart nosedive into an abyss of worry. With my heart racing, I slightly hold my hands up in question…*what gives?*

His contorted face, awash with fresh tears, lies beside me in a crumpled heap of grief. "It's going to be okay. You're strong. You'll fight this! We can go anywhere in the nation, and—"

"It's bad, isn't it?" He silently nuzzles his face against my shoulder. "Remember when you got pissed because I didn't tell you right off I was pregnant? You wanted me to treat you like an adult. Turnabout is fair play. Spill it…how bad? The baby's okay, right?" I impatiently add, "Your bedside manner sucks right now, doctor."

His breath is warm and comforting on my face. I have to make myself concentrate on his words, though, as I'm sinking deeper into a heavy, dreamless sleep. "The baby is great. I monitored the fetal heartbeat the whole time and sat with the radiologist, plus a buddy of mine in a different cohort was there, too. The three of us looked at x-rays and biopsy samples."

"Oh no!" I groan. "*Everyone* saw my boobies!" My laughter is met with a play slap from Fielding who tells me to shut the 'F' up. "Just say the word, Fielding. It's not like we're in church or in front of the kids—too much." I point to my belly.

Collin goes bubbly for a minute but a shadow quickly sets across his face. "That radiologist…Jenna, he's smart as hell." Collin's voice wobbles through his last pronouncement, and I know it's because of the diagnosis he has to deliver. "We looked at the genetic testing—it's triple negative. Your breast cancer can be aggressive. Initially, it responds pretty well to chemo, but if it comes back…chemo isn't great. You made a good decision with the mastectomy. I think they took out a couple lymph nodes. We'll fight it hard with chemo, once you've recovered." His hand around my shoulder feels like a vice grip of hope—a hope that seems more like a golden noose.

And his words are heavy, beaten down with worry and anticipation of the agony he knows awaits me: telling the children I'm not sure I'll be okay, sickness, losing my hair, losing my strength, possibly losing the baby, changes in my body and those in Collin's mind about them, and changes to our lives that will put us all in a freefall, barely hanging on for some shred of decent normalcy. *Stop...I can't think about that now.* The slow drip of the I.V. has programmed my eyes for a slow blink. "No. Not that...I don't want that," I slur.

"Shhhh...I'll work with your oncology team myself. I'll study it. I'll become even better than the best cancer doctor. I will do *anything* and *everything* to keep you with us, to keep you with me until *I* am the one to breathe my last breath." Collin abruptly shifts his tone. His mouth hollows out an open spot beside my ear. "Get ready. I'm coming the fuck back. Wanna know a secret?" His smile is smudgy like a museum watercolor.

"Oh, you have secrets you're keeping from me?" A pang of jealousy as I remember the name—*Lena*—then a sucker punch of deceit squares off with me when I think of the Cheater's Club.

"Only the best ones," he nuzzles me closer. "I know where I'm taking you on our honeymoon, and you'll love it."

"No," I whisper, nearly sunken into sleep. "Now...want...."

"What do you mean? What do you want, babe?" he asks, putting his ear near my mouth. Fielding's face hovers between us and she and Collin exchange concerned expressions.

"I want to get married—now."

Chapter Fourteen: The Beautiful Things

The first time I ever heard the "Start Me Up" song by the Stones, I kept replaying the line about making a grown man cry because at the tender age of fifteen, I just couldn't imagine how in the world a woman could reduce a grown man to tears. Preparing to walk down the aisle for the second time, I figure out exactly how that happens.

Remarriage was never on my radar. Remarriage with a much younger man *and* I'm having his baby…*only* in the smut I read. Remarriage and cancer. Never in a fucking million years. The floor-length navy blue dress with the satin sheath, thigh-high slit, and sheer overlay of cascading ruffles is stunning, even on my frame that's been butchered a bit. It doesn't matter that my tits are non-existent because I'm ready to show my shit, and proud to say I'll be taking none of it from cancer. A little wobbly on my heels with my full belly, Fielding steadies me from behind with her hands on my hips in front of the dressing room mirror.

"The blue really brings out your eyes, and your blonde hair." She hovers behind me so I can't see the tears brimming her eyes.

"What's left of it," I counter, plowing my hand through my platinum blonde pixie with a razor-sheared finish in the back. "Still getting used to it." Speaking to her reflection in the mirror, I warn, "Bitch, if you cry,

I'm gonna punch you." I finish, matter-of-factly, "Do you want to be that person who gets checked by the pregnant bride fighting cancer?"

"I'm sorry, I just…." Fielding heaves tortured breaths in and out of her mouth while her head and face bob back and forth as if they're on a spring. "You are such a fucking badass." She wipes tears and snot from her nose with a paper towel. "I don't know if I can let Collin have you."

She abruptly darts into the bathroom when she hears the door squeak open.

My resolve to keep tear-free is nearly pummeled when Bennett strides in. He is dressed in a navy suit and gunmetal gray tie, tall for his age, I foolishly chide myself for not noticing that he's lost his boyish looks. "Mom." His voice cracks, lost between childhood and the young man who is having to grow up too fast—for me. "Mam-Mam and Poppy just walked in. I hope I got 'em seated in the right spot. I had to remind Poppy what to do…like three times!" He forces a laugh to hide his nerves, and maybe some tears.

"Your Poppy will be fine." I breathe slowly through my nose and exhale through my mouth, trying to calm the jitters that have wracked my entire body. "Be prepared to show him what to do again." An awkward silence passes between us. "You okay? I know I've leaned on you a lot lately. And these shoes will be your test," I joke.

He tightens his jaw, his grin now stoic. "You lean on me as much as you need, okay Mom? I'm good. I can handle it. I'll carry you if I have to," he declares, his lips stretched in a resolute thin smile.

"Gosh…someone raised you right." I hug him and

meet Fielding's red-rimmed eyes with my own. I mouth the word "dammit" to her and she reaches out to lightly blot my face, then brightens with another squeak of the door.

"Mom!" Vi squeezes through the door, trying not to let anyone see in, with Jacob in tow. "You look hot! I'm like *so* glad you don't look like a pretty princess. The hair and dress are snatched!"

Jacob hides his face from me, a sullen little shadow behind Vi. "Jacob, are you going to help Mommy down the aisle? Bennett is going to need your help."

He nods, sharing his thoughts, "Mommy, I'm glad for this day, but I'm sad you have to get married and have cancer. But the good news is that you're happy, and love is great medicine, isn't it?"

"Love is always the best medicine." As I embrace all three of my children, I make eye contact with Fielding, sober eye behind the camera. I know this is going to be my favorite picture of them all.

Bennett flanks me to my left and Jacob flanks me to my right as we prepare to walk down the aisle. Vi is in front of me, proud of her ever-growing chest in her grown-up gown and heels. *She'll be a hellcat,* I think as I watch her sway toward the aisle, her blonde curls reaching to the middle of her back, making all kinds of eye contact with the rubberneckers...she has her mother's confidence. I shake my head and have to laugh. Fielding gives me a look—*the look*—that only besties reserve for one another, and especially now because maybe I'll not be around to tame the hellcat. At least Fielding will have had a little practice.

As Jacob pushes open the dressing room door for us, light strikes through the stained glass transom, showering us with a spotlight that's surely made for this day—*our* day. I slip a hand into the crook of Bennett's arm and another in the crook of Jacob's arm. Vi is behind me, straightening the beaded train of my dress.

"If you start to wobble in your heels, suck in your stomach. It really works," Vi lectures. *Nearly fourteen going on thirty, and dammit, she's right.* "Mom?" she asks.

"What, sweetheart?" *I hope this is a teachable moment...for both of us. I'm probably limited on the number of those I have left.*

"How did you know Collin was the one?"

The processional music is starting, and I cinch like engine oil left idle in the dead of winter. I peek around the massive oak frame of the doorway to see my guests whack-a-mole-turning in all directions, trying to catch the first glimpse of the not-so-princess bride. I'm not sure how to answer Vi because the reality is that the older you get, you realize that important decisions sometimes take a massive leap of faith, and sitting around waiting on a sign or on the moment to feel right is just a time suck. *Carpe diem.*

I let go of the boys for a moment and motion her back to the threshold of the dressing room, hurrying as I hear the second chorus of the music. "For a long time, I wasn't certain of how to know. And to be honest, I'm not sure you can ever be really *sure*. But what I *have* figured out is that you can share from your heart, you can do your best to stay true to yourself and your values, and...I think focus on the positive more than the negative. Remember that you should like the person as much as you love him—and hopefully he feels the same—and you should be able to tell that. If you can't—run."

I playfully tap my finger on my temple and give her a shoulder shrug. "Love isn't complicated with Collin, it's a beautiful mess. That's how I think I really knew."

"Yeah, I can tell he makes you calmer. He makes you the woman I admire and love with all my heart, which is a weird thing to say because, I mean…you're my *mom*, not just a great woman." She hugs me and I breathe her in as much today as I did on the day I brought her into this mean old world.

She whispers, "Kick cancer's ass so that you can be at *my* wedding."

That's my hellcat.

If I drop dead in this moment, my life would be enough because in these precious moments of time, floating on the notes of a song, I see the goodness that I put into the world. Maybe I could have done better, and I sure as hell could have done worse. But, I did my best and it's damn good.

Jumping back to our skein like geese in flight, Fielding paddles down the aisle ahead of us. My heart nearly rattles loose in my chest when I see the smiles and the tears of all the people I love who are here to love me and honor my life. With my teeth chattering and my bouquet shaking, I round the aisle and make eye contact with Collin. He's wearing a simple, tailored navy blue pinstriped suit and the same gunmetal gray tie as Bennett. I lick my lips and give Fielding a look…*the look* because I know she knows what I'm thinking. *He's so fuckable, even at the altar. Yes, I did just think that in church, but my guy—God…he gets me.*

My very-soon-to-be-husband's blue eyes melt me with their teary, starlight sparkle. Even as I scan the crowd, trying to absorb this whole moment, Collin's eyes never abandon my floating-on-air descent down the aisle. At the end of the last pew are my open-armed parents—my mother, winded from what's likely been an exasperating day with my father who is just as winded—but from the knowledge that finally I've found peace in love with a man who he knows cares for me just as much as *he* does. I've done the scrappy fight dance to make it this far—and I'm not even talking about cancer. *I am my father's daughter.* His kiss bids me farewell to my children, who follow me to Collin because…we're a package deal.

We don't surprise anyone with our own iteration of a traditional ceremony, and I deliver my vows with as much loving irreverence as I can without getting us all struck by lightning. "When I first saw you, I *wanted* to assume it was lust, and that it would pass. But as the song goes, 'I fooled around and well…fell in love.'" A chorus of laughter buoys me along. "Maybe on some level I didn't think I needed love, or even deserved it. But what I really discovered about my love for you is that it's forever tied to the love I have for myself and these beautiful children. You've cleanly convicted me of this one lesson I have finally and truly learned: Of all the ways you can express love, the most important way is respect. I will always love you, Collin English, because even when I was out to get me, you stood by ready to scoop me up when I didn't have the strength. And now I know I'll never have to rely on my own strength again."

Collin takes my hands and cups them in his, which are tingly warm. He suddenly breaks into a trembling, teary mess, whispering so that only I can hear, "Oh God, please don't take this away from me!" I clench his hands as hard as I can until he regains his composure, and I have no idea how I don't collapse in a heap of tears, but I don't.

"I knew, I *knew*, the first time I saw you...I was an incomplete man. You're the other half of me—definitely my better half—and definitely the package deal that was the bargain of the century because all I owe you, all of you, is my heart. When people ask me what I did to bag such a babe, I tell 'em not to ask me what I did, but what I didn't do: I didn't try to clip your wings—your sweet, beautiful angel wings."

I recognize my father's suppressed snort; he's trying not to ugly cry because somewhere, long ago, I remember when he sent me to college with that same message and kissed me on the forehead. *Angel wings*. As I turn to look at the loving smiles and misty eyes, I wonder who will be here when I die, and will they be as happy as I will be when I get my angel wings for real? Provided I get them, but like I said...my guy God, he gets me. I may be on probation for a while, hanging at the pearly gates, but I think I can convince him I'd be a good catch.

At the pronouncement, Collin scoops me up in his arms and holds me up, thrilled like the little kid who's just won the prize from the cereal box. Our long passionate kiss is slayed by Fielding, Vi, Jacob, and Bennett piling us with hugs and a tsunami of laughter and cheers from the crowd. The officiant has to bellow over the noise, announcing the words I've been waiting for:

"Loved ones, I am proud to present to you, Mr. and Mrs. Collin English!"

I open my eyes for the cameras that flock us, but it's the brilliant, blinding ray of light piercing the transom that bathes me in peace. I turn to Vi. "This…this is how love should be. Never give up on believing that you deserve the beautiful things in this life."

Chapter Fifteen: Just for Eternity

"Did you ever think you'd see such a sight?" My arms droop at my sides and I strain my neck, my heaving belly pulling me in an opposite direction, stretching to see the top tier of the tower bathed in lights, the mountains hovering behind it, cloaked in a thick fog.

"It's a pretty impressive little reproduction, yeah?" Collin's eyes float to the top with mine. "I know you really wanted to go to Paris. I'll take you there someday, Jenna...when you're done with treatment. I know it doesn't exactly compare, but not bad for Paris...*Tennessee*, right? I mean it's kinda cool...a tiny Eiffel Tower. Plus, it's close to a hospital...just in case."

"I'm gonna require an I.O.U." I smirk.

Collin high fives me, with a folding finish, his fingers over mine. "You ready to go back to the cabin? If we hurry we can watch the birds fly in on the lake. They say it's amazing."

Nuzzling behind my ear, he whispers, "I'll make some fresh roasted salmon and potatoes, a nice little salad, butter up some of that good sourdough we picked up from the Mennonite store, and maybe we can have a bedroom dessert, if you're up to it?" He spins me around and offers me a toothy grin like an earnest emoji.

I answer with a vacant stare across the lake as the geese land in pairs, pushing Collin away as I approach the shore. "I'm afraid to make love to you. This will be the first time since the surgery."

He's at my heels. "Why? I told you that doesn't matter to me."

"My scars. You'll be disgusted, repulsed. Maybe you'll secretly want someone else, and it will gnaw at you until…"

"Until I cheat?"

"People cheat for all kinds of reasons. That's one of them. I'm not naïve about it. I think I look kinda freakish. You didn't sign up for this when you proposed."

"I know the *story* behind your scars, and cheating isn't going to be a part of that story."

"You haven't seen them yet." I pull the tabs of my collar together.

Collin sweeps my hands away. "I don't need to see them because all I can see is you. And that's all I want, all I need."

I rest my hands on my belly while he continues to press the corners of my collar flat. He moves to the first, then second and third buttons. I suck in a steadying breath, and his wandering hands leave my teeth chattering. "I'm not sure I'm ready," I whisper with my eyes closed.

"Shhhh." He slides his index finger over my cheekbones and lips. "Just keep your eyes on me. I don't need to look. I just wanna touch you a little tonight…my wife. The brave warrior woman I love…I'll always love."

The short lapping of the dark water on the shore fills my ears. Night music—crickets, a bullfrog, and the distant crying of a coyote—is the love song his hands use to serenade my body to do his will. I stand in front of him, trying to find his eyes in the dark; I hunt for his body to steady myself. Much of the area is still numb. It's not erotic, this kind of touching, yet my mind swoons and swirls at his fingertips, memories of our bodies, *my* body, before the surgery. His hot breath comes in waves on my ear and I grimace, wanting to know what thoughts he's allowing to circulate in his mind.

"Let's go," he exhales, as I let his humid mix of mint and bourbon coax me to the cabin.

The fifty or so feet we walk in silence, an owl hoots his hushed warning and Collin drapes a fresh quilt over the porch chaise, trolling me into the sacred spot between his arms, my head resting at his heart as I slide his ring off and on his finger. "I know you worry, but I need you to just hear me out. Sometimes, love comes into your life to teach you lessons, and sometimes it comes in as a bridge to something different or better. And then, if you're really lucky, there's love that will find you and *change* you, if you let it, if you're not foolish. Let me love you the way you are, Jenna. Let me prove to you that I only want you, and I only need you for a little while—just for eternity."

A smile he can't see plies my face in the dark. "Well, okay, but that's not for very long."

****

Reality is a bitch.

It's week thirty-one.

Chemotherapy begins with Fielding knocking at my door—6 a.m. I rip it open and immediately put my fingers to my lips. "What the hell are you doing? The appointment isn't until 8:30!" My words slice through the air and her face deflates.

"I brought coffee and your favorite pastry from that little French bakery you love. I wanted to sit on the deck and have coffee with you, watch the sun rise—and gab. It's one of my favorite things." Her eyes strongarm tears that want to be rescued.

"I'm sorry. I'm up…have been for an hour or so. I'd love that, Fielding."

Fielding keeps her back to me. She sniffles and I watch a tear drip off the end of her nose as she busies herself with making me a plate. "Hey, Fielding." I try to stand but the weight of my belly throws me off balance and I immediately sink back into the chair. "I'm sorry. I'm…all over the place this morning."

"Yeah." She drapes a napkin over my lap and tucks one into my shirt, pressing it over my belly. "I know how you are." Her mouth twists up to one side.

"Fielding?"

"Yeah?"

"I don't tell you nearly enough, and hell, maybe I haven't told you at all. I'm so lucky to have found you, sweet friend. A lot of people go through their adult lives essentially alone—not any real go-to person, feeling like…I don't know…like they're floating through their lives on this precarious thread that might break, and who will catch them? I'm so lucky, so blessed because I know exactly who will catch me."

"You better know it! Although, I couldn't exactly catch your fat ass right now." Her beautiful dark eyes rake over me like hot coals.

"Come sit beside my big fat ass, friend, while you still can." I pat the seat beside me, and she squeezes in.

The sun teases us from behind the rain clouds, which doesn't deter us from enjoying our morning coffee and conversation. The only interruption is the gate creaking open and Fielding's breath suddenly clutching from suppressing a cry. The soft padding of feet and a familiar voice—one that's eluded me for too long.

Cliff lumbers around the corner cradling a paper bag with a big greasy spot on the side. He murmurs to Fielding, "When you weren't at home, I remembered about today. I thought you all might like some breakfast before you go. It's one of your favorites—there's enough for two." Cliff's eyes float to meet Fielding's.

With Fielding's silence fueling the awkwardness, I chime in. "Cliff! I'm so happy to see you! It's been too long. Is that Lancaster's biscuits and sausage gravy?" I push myself up and waddle toward him.

He hands off the bag to me, the brown paper crumpled with sweat from his hands. "How are you, Jenna?" He fumbles around my belly at the embrace, holding me longer than I want to hold him, his fingers digging into and clinging to my ribs for a desperate moment. "Congratulations are in order, and I'll skip the obvious condolences because nobody could give a damn chance to fate's ruin with this lady riding shotgun." He bobs his head toward Fielding, who holds up a chocolate-hazelnut-filled croissant.

"I brought Jenna's favorite. I was thinking about her."

Cliff's tender voice warbles his reply. "I was thinking of you. I knew today would be hard on you. If you need me, I'm here."

Fielding shrugs him off, tearing open the bag with her back to him.

"Cliff, why don't you go inside and grab a cup of coffee…join us. There's enough for *three*," I say loudly.

Once safely inside I swipe at Fielding with a plastic fork. "What the hell? Why are you giving him such a cold shoulder, huh? That was incredibly sweet of him, and he did it for *you*. I'll bet he had to stand in line for an hour to get this," I lecture, scooping up a soggy spoonful of the peace offering into my mouth. "This is good, right? It's forward movement, right?"

"I guess." She runs her finger through the gravy on my plate, licking it off, playfully watching for Cliff.

"You don't have to make a decision or do anything, Fielding, except maybe give the poor guy a chance. Doesn't he deserve a chance?"

"I had kinda given up on him trying to win me back."

"Well, your knight in shining armor may be late, but at least he brought gifts." Her brown eyes cut across the plate suspiciously. "He got you the extra gravy, Fielding. *Who* else will remember your extra gravy?"

We settle at the table, an orange sherry sunrise draping the three of us in warmth. Fielding brushes the sniffles back from her nose and smiles to herself, her mouth collapsing around a spoonful of milk gravy, closing her eyes and enjoying the moment of thought that maybe her knight in shining armor had actually come through.

"I love watching you enjoy that," Cliff whispers.

"Are you trying to come on to me?" Fielding asks, deep in mid-chew.

He leans over and wipes the corner of her mouth with a napkin. "Maybe, but I just really like seeing you happy. And I really like that I was the one who made you smile—for a change."

"Don't be a dolt. It wasn't you. It was the Lancaster's biscuits and gravy." Fielding leans into him until she's nose to nose, commanding his mouth to open for the bite of breakfast she's willing to share.

Cliff laughs and blows on the fork. "I love your snarky bits." His besotted stare drills a hole through her that I could feel in my *own* panties. "I'm free today," he offers, his words warbling at mid-chew. "The kids are at STEM camp. I thought I could drive you. Would you let me? It can feel like a miserable eternity…at a hospital, just *waiting*."

"I'll be nurse-ratcheding I suppose," Fielding glares at me and I shrug, shaking my head in agreement with his plan, "but if you'd like to be the chauffeur," she considers, "I guess you could do that."

"I'll do whatever you want, Fielding." Cliff exhales, his words landing steady and sticking a near-perfect score in Fielding's judgment. She suddenly stands with her back to us and snatches the paper plates and bags, plastic silverware, and napkins—mashing everything together in a kaleidoscope ball of worry. Cliff saunters over to her so that she's forced to look at him, and he removes the ball from her hand, carelessly tossing it back on the table.

"I don't need your—"

She doesn't finish her sentence because Cliff puts his mouth on hers while raking his fingers through her hair, holding her captive in the small of her back. "I know you don't need me, and I want to change that—need me like the air you breathe, Fielding." He leans in toward her again, his mouth falling over hers as she pushes her palms—hard—into his chest, finally giving in to his kiss, wobbling on her wedge heels and recovering with a fingertip balance on the edge of the table.

She says nothing. Her face is rosy and shimmering. She makes no gestures other than sobbing crescendos to wailing and then…the comfort of his arms and shoulders muffles her emotion.

Reality might be a bitch, but she's a bitch with a wicked sense of humor.

"So, interrupting right now would be so shitty because no one wants to see how this plays out more than me, but I think I'm going to need to get to the hospital sooner rather than later."

"I've never heard of anyone *asking* to go to their chemo appointment," Cliff mumbles, his hands cradling Fielding's face like a love struck teenager.

"I'm asking to go to the hospital because my water broke," I lecture, moaning at the last bite of biscuits and gravy.

"Your water broke? Now?" Fielding drops to her knees to verify. "It's not time yet! The baby's early…too early!"

"Go wake up Collin!" I holler, blowing through the first contraction.

Fielding and Cliff run into the house hand-in-hand like they did on the way home from a campus Bob Dylan concert decades ago when I watched them run ahead, zigzagging across the sidewalk to Beatnick Burgers, so in love not just with each other, but with life itself. *Maybe love doesn't have an expiration date. Maybe less-than-perfect love can rise out of the ashes as something different, and maybe even something better. Maybe this will be Fielding and Cliff's phoenix love story.*

And what will this be for me? I refuse to believe that this moment is anything except what it's supposed to be—*joyful.* I put one hand on my heart and the other on my baby. *We're in this together—all of it. No matter how long I'm here, I'll always be with you. I'll always be here*

for you—even when reality is a bitch.
****

"I can deliver this baby if I have to," Collin reassures me, donning his lab coat and wrapping the stethoscope around his neck. "Hopefully we can stop the labor at the hospital." Collin lifts me into the back seat of Fielding's car and to Collin's back, she flexes her bicep then makes a heart shape with her hands while shaking her chest at him with a perfectly pursed pucker. She never wastes a sexy moment and that's something I'll never tire of, no matter how inappropriate the situation.

Fielding snorts. "I can deliver vomit. Lots of vomit if you have to do that, Doctor. Please do not do that in my car," she calls to the back seat.

I sucker punch the back of her seat and grunt, moaning and panting through a contraction. Resting my head on Collin's shoulder, I squeeze his hands in mine, staving off the end of the contraction.

"Gooo! Fielding! Drive, dammit!" Collin booms, ducking his head between the front seats and pointing at the windshield.

Fielding calmly turns to Cliff, commenting, "You ever notice how a baby coming out sounds a lot like a baby being made, going in? Don't you find that interesting? What do you think of that, Dr. English? Why do those moans sound the same? Is that a question for a qualified medical professional?" She grips the steering wheel and fishtails out of the driveway, proving that comedy and crisis are pulsing and alive and well in her blood.

I grab the head rest and laugh until I'm peeing fluid again. "It sure doesn't *feel* as good coming out as going in though!" I cackle.

"For sure," she agrees, blowing through a red light, ignoring the sirens suddenly blaring behind us.

"What the hell are you doing?" Collin yells. "There's a cop back there!"

"I'm getting you to the hospital! What does it look like I'm doing? Don't worry. I've got maneuvers. I'll wave him on so he'll know it's an emergency." Fielding adjusts her mirrors again and adjusts herself in her seat, her body nearly pressed into the steering wheel.

Collin rests his head on my shoulder and mumbles something about all of us dying or going to jail. "It's okay," I pant, blowing through another contraction, thinking of something to distract him. "Eight weeks early and a girl…that's the best case scenario for being early, right?"

"She'll fare better than a boy. She may be a little small, but her lungs will be stronger, and you're healthy, plus you've had a pretty normal pregnancy…except—"

He's interrupted by Fielding hollering out the window at the police officer who is riding at her side. "Holy mother of God! We have an emergency here, sir!"

"If you're going to break the law, then break it! Go, Fielding, go!" Collin pumps his fist in the air and she punches the accelerator, nearly missing the entrance to the hospital, and thankfully, a man on his walker out for a smoke.

By this time, I know my contractions are close enough together that there's no putting a stop to this baby making an appearance; Fielding is sitting on the curb, handcuffed and holding a smile precariously close to pleasure. As Collin helps me into the wheelchair, she gives me a wink, and shimmies her eyebrows up and down, cocking her head toward Cliff, who is arguing with the officer about rendering aid and emergencies. "Push it *real* good!" She sings the popular riff to a song from when we were kids and I call back to her, "There's no other way I'd have this baby! You in handcuffs, me with cancer, oh, and the police! What could be more perfect?"

The only thing that could be more perfect is the arrival of Delilah Rose English.

I watch Collin hold his daughter, almost five and a half pounds of everything that he believes is the key to his happiness, and what he doesn't know yet—the tiny maker of everything that can be exhilaratingly crushing. I keep that secret, a Mona Lisa smile plied to my face; he looks like a kid with a new toy. "Did you ever think you could fall in love with another human so quickly?"

"Well, yeah. I mean her mom made quick work of me." He grins, cradling Delilah to his chest. His face suddenly sours and he tucks the baby into her bassinet. "You know, you've delayed the chemo until you just can't anymore."

"Technically, this delay wasn't me. I didn't plan it." I hold up a burp cloth as my white flag of surrender.

Collin's right eyebrow high steps across the creases on his forehead. "I think you two probably colluded to get your way."

He settles himself beside me on the bed and clears his throat. "You can take two weeks off and then you've got to start it. Jenna. Please, I know you don't want to, but I need you to...for me, for Vi, for Jacob, for Bennett, for your parents, for Fielding. For Delilah. I don't care why you do it, just start. Don't you want to be here to enjoy all the moments with all the people you love? But you've thought about that, right? You haven't given up,

right?"
Right.
Reality is a bitch.

Chapter Sixteen: Just Call Me...a Cheater

Delilah will be almost a year old when I finish all of my chemotherapy treatments. She'll be crawling, smiling and laughing, eating mostly solid food, she might even be able to say 'momma' or 'dada.' It will be a year of her life she'll likely not remember, and one that I'll never forget.

"I don't want to count down treatments or ring bells or anything like that," I announce when Fielding brings in a big wall calendar. "I want events."

"Okay," Fielding hesitates and glances at Collin, "whatever. Do you have some ideas I could work with?"

"When I finish a treatment, I want to do something ordinary with someone I love. I want to build good memories around all this. Not bad ones. For example, when I finish the first treatment, I want you to bring me a Beatnik Burger. Remember we'd go grab a big greasy double decker after partying all night—"

"Babe, I love the idea," Collin interrupts, "but you gotta be careful about eating anything that could make you sick. Remember, your immune system, along with your digestive system, will be kinda trashed for a while. And you'll feel nau—"

"Okay!" I snap, crossing my arms on my chest. "I get it! How about some tasteless gruel with the man I love?" I roll my eyes, the baby fidgeting on my lap, ready for her bottle. "I guess I can only enjoy feeding her for a little while longer, too, huh?" I pick her up and watch her newborn scrunch, kissing her little chubby cheek. "I can't handle her once I start chemo."

"You can, but you'll have to wait until you feel better. That's the goal: our whole focus, our mission because without you, our world will shatter, Jenna."

"See, all these rules and recommendations. I don't want it to be like this," I whine, annoyed with my own voice and frustration. "There's got to be a compromise, right?"

After one of the first treatments, Collin makes his own smash burgers, carefully cooked, for an audience of one, and in nothing but an apron. He even delivers it to me in bed with his awkward stripper moves. I couldn't finish the burger, or even begin on him, but I guarantee I'll remember it every time I eat all-beef patties—or see his buns. *Wink. Wink.*

Fielding takes me to sit in the sun at a butterfly sanctuary with the best (and only) tart cherry mocktail I've ever had. She "fixed" hers with some rum. *Of course she did.*

The kids, Collin, Fielding, Cliff, and their kids pack me and my chemo snacks on a mattress in the back of my van and we go to see a movie at the drive in. Delilah and I snuggle and sleep on and off during the whole thing, but I wake to laugh at the best parts with the kids.

I am determined to see Bennett graduate, and on his way out one afternoon, I tug at his arm and pull at the skin on my head. "I know your old mom looks like a hairless chihuahua, but will I embarrass you if I go?" I sheepishly ask him.

Bennett strokes the peach fuzz on his chin and warmly touches my head. "I'd be devastated if you didn't go, no matter what you look like. I love you, Mom!" He gives me a tight squeeze around my chest and bounds out the door.

At graduation, the valedictorian announces that his speech will be abbreviated because he wants to give the floor to someone with an important message. Bennett rises from the crowd and approaches the stage, along with a string of his friends who stand behind him. They are all bald underneath their caps.

"One of the things you learn in school from a very early age is how to overcome obstacles. Maybe you start with the playground bully and progress to recovering from your first bad grade or trying to still look cool when you're turned down by your crush. Or maybe it's trying to find your way after graduation. Whatever it may be, learning to walk away or how to stay and fight, and fight well, is only possible with the strength of love.

"A lot of you know that my mom is fighting cancer, but that's not what I want to discuss. I want to talk about her strength and grace. She's a hero when she's scared. She's always there for support, even when she's weak. I hate that my mom has cancer, but if it's taught me anything, it's this: Never stop giving people a reason to fight for love. There will always be something that will vie for your attention and your passion. Make sure that you always pick the beautiful things, the things that make love worth fighting for. I love you, Mom."

And that moment, I began to realize the worth of my presence. *I need to really and truly live.*

And the moment after that, I am surrounded by all the people I love, sprawled on the floor with my heart buzzing in my ears.

Fight.

****

"Hey…Fielding. Baby! It's okay. It's *okay.* Why don't you take a break? Get some hot tea, some fresh air, and a little walk. I'm here." It sounds like Cliff is digging in his pocket for something. "Here, take a five and make a meal out of the vending machine. You still like that, right?"

"I'm glad you're here," she whispers through her slow roll of tears that still strangles her words. "I thought maybe we'd lost her."

"She's been fighting hard. Collin said it's a minor setback. It's normal for white blood counts to drop." He rattles loose change in his pockets hunting for words.

"Uhm…are you glad I'm here?" he asks, popping and crunching the bill between his fingers.

"Cliff, you know what I realized? It won't matter how I feel six months from now, or even six years from now. I was so damn mad at you. I wanted to get your attention, to shock you, to show you I was still a woman who wants you to *need me.* Hell, I even tried to cheat on you, but…"

"Fielding, I wouldn't blame you, but happy as hell that you didn't. I'm sorry I didn't change enough, quickly enough. I was angry and immature about it. I didn't want to accept that maybe I needed to take some responsibility for things. I'm an asshole."

"You still are, and always will be, but that's not why I didn't." She delivers the zinger and adds, "And not because I love you," she continues coyly.

I summon my strength to crank my eyelids open and see that Fielding has moved to Cliff's lap and she's got his determined jaw resting in her hands. "Why do you love me, Fielding?"

"I love you because you—*you* are my story. You are heartbeats and kisses, and babies laughing and crying in weeks-on-end sleepless nights, and sweet or sexy secrets only we know, and burned dinners and shrunken, mismatched socks, binge watching home improvement shows, and tears and terrible lies, and the crazy uncertainty of life, and the changes that make me afraid of nothing but death. You're right here, right now. You are the one man, the *only* man, who healed me by loving me at my best and my worst. You loved me for *me.* And I forgot that, which actually makes *me* the asshole, but I'll never admit it again. So, I hope you got that on your phone or something."

I keep my eyes tightly crimped to stave off the tears, and I know this for sure: Fielding just really made me proud to be her best friend.

And the next thing that I know for sure pummels my heart even more than watching love for the win.

I am dying.

****

Collin clenches my hand vice-grip style as we stare at x-rays and listen to the oncologist spill out details that mean little because in the end…the game is almost over for me, and it'll be a clincher. Collin believes that the stronger he holds me, the lesser the odds of losing me. I squeeze back as hard as I can. I watch him fight back the ripple of tears. *But, that's not how it works.*

"The cancer has advanced, far more than I could ever have anticipated." Dr. Gregg stumbles across his discovery, adding, "It's unusual, the way this cancer is behaving, but not unheard of. The good news is that you responded well to the chemo, so we can hit it again, after we go in with radiation first."

"Wow. So, what the hell is the bad news?"

Dr. Gregg plays with the hem on his lab coat, considering his words, flicking the tip of the pen in and out. "You're at stage four. Basically, you'll have lifetime maintenance chemo and a couple medications to keep your hormones from feeding it. All we can do is keep the cancer at bay, under control enough to keep you…"

"Alive?"

Dr. Gregg nods at me, trading his pen back and forth between his fingers, avoiding making eye contact with Collin. "You know…lots of people live a long time at stage four. It doesn't have to be a finality. Adherence to medication protocol, living a healthy lifestyle, a positive outlook…"

"How long?" Collin stumbles over his words, his red-rimmed eyes burn with determination. I had expected him to ask questions that I didn't understand, not the one that has burned a jagged hole through my brain for months and months.

Dr. Gregg shifts on the stool and randomly scrolls through my file with the stylus. He rolls back against the wall with a sharp exhale. "Man, I've been doing this a long time. I've seen it all—people who meet the average, people who die within a week of walking out of here, people who live longer than I ever believed they would. I could give you a number—five years." His wild eyes watch his hands jump haphazardly in the air. "That's the average at this point. But, honestly, who the hell really knows? You understand, as well as I do, that everybody is different and how you care for yourself, your support system—all the things we little scientists can't actually measure, but desperately want to—make a huge impact."

Dr. Gregg then rolls his seat directly in front of

Collin and rests a tired hand on his drooping shoulders. "The hardest things to learn, they don't teach you in medical school, or even in your residency. You learn those things from your patients, *if* you're a good doctor. So, a long time ago, a woman told me not to try and figure out—or even to consider—why some people get their wings early, before we think they're ready. Some people just do. If I had to give you one piece of advice to extend her life, it would be this: Love her the best you can. The human body is remarkable, resilient, but one thing it can't live without is love."

"I can't live without her," Collin stammers, uncertainty strangling his hope, watching the sun burn frost off of the trees. In the far distance, the outline of the Cumberland Mountains guard a smudgy gray sky, and I notice a snow squall inching closer to the valley of Kinweld. A Bible verse pounds in my brain: *Though I walk through the valley of the shadow of death.*

****

You helped me uncover the hope that I had given up trying to find.

That was the line, the *only* line, I managed to write in what I thought might be my final letter, the letter that someone would have read at my funeral. But…I kept coming back to Bennett's face and his words at graduation; Vi's question at the wedding; and Jacob's words about love being the best medicine—surely, a little boy's heart can't be wrong, right?

So, I fought like hell. *Because I wanted to truly live…and I had hope. Hell, I still even had a little confidence.*

I cried. I screamed. I got mad, depressed, hopeless, and felt like an imposter. I puked, I went bald, I endured the weirdest, shittiest experiments—things bodies shouldn't have to go through. I clung in fear to the people I loved; I pushed them away in disgust and self-loathing. I guided Jacob through to beginning middle school. I helped Vi do her hair for her first high school dance. I accompanied Bennett to college visit day. I potty trained Delilah. I was maid of honor in Fielding's vow renewal ceremony. And I watched Collin accept a position as an attending at a local family practice office. The first day of his first physician's job, he got a complementary blow job. *I'm not that sick.*

After almost eighteen months, I dragged my frazzled, tattered body in for a scan and bloodwork with Dr. Gregg. Collin sat beside me, clamping his hand over mine, the same vice-grip style, hoping beyond hope for some decent news. *And where is my confidence now?*

"Don't get too excited. Whatever it is, it is. Okay?" I hunt his eyes for hope that has metastasized outside of our reality.

"I know I promised never to clip your wings, but I really want to." Collin pulls his sweaty hands away from me, wiping them on his jeans. "I have a good feeling. I think you've beaten it."

I twist my wedding band around on my finger and let my mind wander to Elizabeth. *Whatever happened to her and her Cheater's Club?* A timid smile creeps across my face and Collin catches it like a third base hail Mary.

"What're you grinning about, sexy lady?" He nudges my shoulder with his.

I pause and consider his question...*truth versus dare...do I dare tell him the truth? Not every truth will set you free.* "I'm just thinking," I push my body into his and give him a sultry peck on his lips, holding it there, "what a silly fool I was—being unsatisfied with our life together. I wish I'd just…pushed through, leaned in, had a change of heart earlier, a different perspective sooner. You know?"

"I'm not sorry." He stares into my eyes without blinking, a fire in the future he wants with me. "If neither one of us hadn't been in the place we were, I don't think we'd be as strong as we are now. I never have regrets with you—no matter what. And don't you have regrets either. No matter what."

I tuck my head under his chin and repeat his words, "No matter what."

The click of the door handle startles us both and Dr. Gregg slogs through the room to his stool. His eyes hold a pair of dark circles and his usual smile is a scowl. He rattles off pleasantries more like dreaded requirements, and the smell of day-old coffee and worn grief looms over us. He clicks on his laptop, scrolling through the file with a mad hilarity. A series of *hmmms* and *uhs* pop out of his mouth in machine-gun fashion.

"Have you looked in your patient portal yet?" he asks, a grin slowly soaking his face.

"I stay out of the patient portal for my own mental health."

"Well," Dr. Gregg's words are stuck in the indecipherable gutter of his throat, "Your scans. Your blood work. Everything. They all point to your being in remission. You were in stage four, and now you're in remission."

He balls up his fist and holds it against his upper lip. "Before I came in here, I had to tell a man he had three months—and that was generous. Two nights ago, I lost a patient—a young guy with kids. The past few weeks…that's been my job, my life—telling people they're on the path toward death. And it's killing me."

Dr. Gregg folds his hand over his eyes like a visor, shielding him from the bright reality. "Jenna, you did it. You're an honorary member."

"An honorary member?" I twist around to Collin who is as confused as I am.

"We oncologists have a name for people who defy the odds, who beat the disease. You're a member of the Cheater's Club."

Well, I'll be damned…and blessed. I wish Fielding could be here to hear this shit. I'm an honorary member…the Cheater's Club. Better yet, if only Elizabeth knew….

"She's cheated death," the half-formed words fumble out of Collin's open lips.

"Damn right I did—and no regrets. No matter what."

A word about the author...

Stella Grae is an unassuming English professor, copyeditor, and copywriter living in Lexington, Kentucky. She's the author of the novelette "DOMcember" and the erotic romance novel Just Call Me Confidence. In her spare time she enjoys sipping on bourbon, nibbling cheesy grits, and philosophizing about love and sex in her blog, "Bone Up," which can be found on her website: stellagraeerotica.weebly.com…along with other sexy tidbits.

stellagraeerotica.weebly.com

Thank you for purchasing
this publication of The Wild Rose Press, Inc.

For questions or more information
contact us at
info@thewildrosepress.com.

The Wild Rose Press, Inc.
www.thewildrosepress.com